LAID IN EARTH

Josef Slonský Investigations Book Six

Graham Brack

SAPERE
BOOKS

LAID IN EARTH

Published by Sapere Books.

20 Windermere Drive, Leeds, England, LS17 7UZ,
United Kingdom

saperebooks.com

ISBN: 978-1-913335-87-8

Chapter 1

Hanuš Himl loaded his barrow once more and laboriously reversed it out of the greenhouse before turning it around so he could get back to the flower bed on which he was currently working.

Hanuš loved his job, and he particularly enjoyed it when spring came around and he could be creative, though he would not have used the word. The budget that he was given to manage the gardens he tended was hopelessly insufficient, but one of the wonderful things about plants was that you could take cuttings and hence keep up a supply even without money, so Hanuš had been busy dividing, cutting, rooting and generally mollycoddling his babies all through the winter and now he was ready to start introducing them to the outside world.

The first thing he had to do was to break up the top layers of soil just in case there was still ice underneath, so last week he had taken a fork to the flower beds. It did not take long if you knew what you were doing and worked steadily, which was just as well, because Hanuš had a lot of gardens to look after and not much in the way of help.

Hanuš was an orderly man, and systematically loaded his barrow in the order that the plants would have to come off: those in the centre of the beds first, then working outwards to the margins. It was his habit to place the trays on the earth for a while before planting so that the plants could get used to their new surroundings. After all, he would say, we don't just take children to a new school and throw them in through the door. We give them some time to get used to a place and make some new friends.

On this particular morning, he had planned to plant five beds that ran down the southern edge of the site in a horseshoe shape. Each barrow would carry about half a bedful of plants, so he made a number of trips to lay out the first couple.

It was then that he noticed something odd about the third bed. He knew these places intimately. He had handled the soil for years. And though he could not immediately tell you what was wrong, it took him no time at all to decide that there was something strange here.

He did what he had always done at times of perplexity. He upturned a bucket and sat on it while he thought. In the old days he would have had a smoke, but he had cut that out once he realised that it was affecting his whistling, so he sat and whistled a tune or two while he looked at the flower bed and tried to decide what to do next.

Having given it due consideration, he settled on the best course of action. He would finish beds one and two, then he would tackle five and four, and he would leave number three until tomorrow. In the meantime he would go to a bar to see if that big fellow was there, the one who was something to do with the police. Josef Slonský.

He had shared quite a few happy hours with Slonský, sipping beer and talking about the old days, not that either of them was starry-eyed about the past. The policeman worried that if young people weren't reminded of what the past had really been like, the many little inconveniences and injustices that filled your days, they might head back that way again. Things like the "voluntary" extra hours you put in on holidays, or the nepotism that saw people promoted far beyond their merits, or simply the lies.

It was the bare-faced lying that had niggled Hanuš. The news reports that had described bumper crops when anyone with eyes could see they were not doing well; the stories they had been fed of food riots in London and New York that turned out to be baffling news to tourists from those places; Hanuš particularly remembered how the head of the Australian Communist Party had been feted by the press, which was a bit of a shock to visiting Australians who didn't even know Australia had a Communist Party, and were pretty definite that it was not on the point of taking power, whatever *Rudé Právo* claimed on its front page.

Hanuš slapped his knee as if to seal the decision, inverted his bucket once more, and got on with his day. That man Slonský was the answer. He would know what to do for the best.

Hanuš pushed open the door and looked inside the pub, taking a few moments to accommodate his eyes to the gloom. For a moment he thought he was out of luck, then he spotted the familiar bulky figure in the tatty overcoat standing at the far end of the bar, a large glass of beer in his hand and a plate of beer cheese in front of him.

It was not the sort of place where there was sport blaring out of television screens. Neither Slonský nor Hanuš would have frequented it if it had been, though they might watch pictures if the sound was turned down. They were content to talk to people who talked to them, and they each knew enough people by sight not to have to pass an evening in silence.

Hanuš slalomed his way through the customers until he was able to slide into a space on Slonský's right side. They greeted each other and Hanuš ordered a beer. It wasn't until he had taken a long pull at his drink, sighed deeply and expressed satisfaction that he felt the conversation could start.

'That first mouthful is worth waiting for,' he said.

'The best,' agreed Slonský. 'It never wears off.'

'Could I ask you a question? Professionally, that is.'

'Of course. But I don't know what your profession is.'

'I'm a gardener,' said Hanuš.

'I guessed that,' answered Slonský. 'The muddy knees and the earthy smell give it away a bit.'

'It's a garden-related question.'

'Not something I know a lot about, but try me.'

Hanuš took another long slurp. 'I look after the gardens for some municipal buildings, and I was working in one today.'

'Would I know it?'

'It's owned by the Ministry of Education, Youth and Sports. Something to do with teacher training, I think. But to people of our age it was more familiar as the Red House.'

Slonský's ears twitched. If you had been an adult in Prague before communism collapsed you would have heard of the Red House. It had been built in the late nineteenth century as the Prague home of some baron or other with more money than taste. Its great attraction was the high walls and large gardens that meant you could shut the world out. After the First World War it had been some sort of sanatorium for a while, and then it had been sequestered for use as a government guest house once the communists came to power.

The guest houses were the regime's answer to hotels for people they required to come to Prague from the provinces. This arrangement had the twin advantages that it left the relatively small number of serviceable hotels free for foreigners with hard currency, and it meant the regime always knew what their country cousins were saying about them because every room was bugged. This was much more convenient than having to install microphones at short notice.

The Red House was a slightly unusual guest house because nobody ever wanted to book in there. It was described as a guest house, looked like a guest house, and bore signage declaring it to be a guest house. More realistically, it was an interrogation centre for the StB, the state's security force.

Most Praguers knew that if you went to Pankrác, that was prison. Bad things might happen to you there, but the Red House existed for the purpose of having bad things happen to people.

When the communist regime broke down there had been calls for the demolition of the Red House as a way of burying the evil memories associated with it. Instead, the new government had decided to devote it to the more cheerful use of training primary school teachers. The inside had been tidied up, the more obvious apparatus of torture had been removed (though you can't remove a stairwell down which victims had been dropped on the end of an elastic rope, never quite knowing if the rope was designed to stop their fall before they reached the floor or not) and with a lick of paint and some brightly coloured vinyl flowers attached to the walls, it had become repurposed to its new use.

'I remember the Red House,' said Slonský. 'Never been inside, I'm pleased to say, but I know what it was.'

'Grim place,' agreed Hanuš, 'but lovely gardens, even if I say so myself. Good soil, you see. It makes all the difference.'

'I'm assuming you're not going to ask me about fertiliser.'

'No, it's more something that I've seen that puzzles me, and I don't know whether to report it. And, if I do, who I need to report it to.'

Hanuš finished his drink, signalled for another and asked Slonský if he wanted one by the silent method of pointing into the glass and raising an eyebrow. Slonský drained the glass in mute acceptance.

'Do you believe the dead come back?' Hanuš asked.

To his credit, Slonský took the question seriously. 'I've never known it. Back in the day a few villains with a noose round their necks used to threaten to come back, but none of them ever did to my knowledge. Why, have you seen someone dead?'

'No, not as such. But I need to let you in on a secret. So far as I can make out, the folks who ran the Red House tried not to kill people there. They would interrogate them, then pass them on to other places for punishment. But I suppose once in a while someone couldn't take the treatment. My predecessor said he sometimes turned up odd bones in the garden at the back. Well, there's a certain flower bed on the south side that I dug over a couple of days ago.' He took a reflective mouthful from his glass and paused to compose the next part of his story. 'You have to be quite sure the ground has thawed deep down before you plant, and it's my habit to fork a bit of manure in as well. Just to give the plants a bit of a start. Anyway, I don't work on Sundays, you know, it's not right. Sunday is a family day. So when I went back this morning, something caught my eye and I can't explain it. The middle bed was higher than the others.'

'Are you fussy about that sort of thing?' said Slonský, fairly sure that he knew what the answer was going to be.

'A garden that's not balanced isn't right,' Hanuš answered. 'You'd see that the soil in that bed was out of line with the others.'

'I wouldn't,' said Slonský. 'You would.'

'I'd always know,' said Hanuš. 'It would offend my sense of order. I'm sure I didn't leave it like that.' He leaned closer to lower his voice. 'And there's another thing. The soil's all wrong.'

Slonský's glass hovered halfway to his mouth. 'How do you mean, wrong?'

'It's the wrong way up. I dig down so far and turn it over and bring the lower stuff to the top. But on this bed it's been turned again, so some of the earth that was originally on the top is now back on the top.'

'You're personally acquainted with each piece of soil, are you?'

Hanuš tutted. 'Any gardener would know. It's been dug over again.'

'So, if I'm safe in assuming there aren't any gangs of secret gardeners sneaking around on the weekend digging over other people's gardens without a by your leave, it's your idea that somebody has been hiding something there.'

'Well, if they didn't bring extra soil, they've put something in the flower bed that has pushed the soil up a few centimetres. Mind, this is a relatively new bed. We only created it last year because it looked unbalanced coming up the west drive with plenty of flowers to your left and none to your right.'

Slonský pondered for a few moments, sank the rest of his beer and ordered two more. 'Tell you what — why don't I come over to the Red House tomorrow morning and see for myself? And we might do a bit of digging.'

Hanuš smiled. He knew he could rely on this fellow.

Chapter 2

Slonský stepped off the bus and strolled through the gates into the garden.

'Beautiful morning,' said Hanuš.

'Beautiful?' Slonský replied. 'When I get back to the city centre, I'm going to have a look under St Wenceslas' horse to see if anything's dropped off in this cold.'

'It's fresh, I'll grant you,' Hanuš answered, 'but it's dry. This way.'

He led Slonský up the drive to the point in front of the main door where the path forked north and south. The building was an odd one. Originally aligned east-west, the addition of a wing and the decision to close the main west door and use doors in the north and south sides to enter the respective corridors gave it a straggly look.

Slonský had heard of the ways it had facilitated secrecy in the past. Respectable guests had been taken to the north door, whereas involuntary visitors were pushed in through the south door. The room in the very south-east corner was particularly remembered by those involuntary guests, because it was only a metre square and had a door with a big rubber seal. At the flick of a switch, it could be filled with the contents of the bath and toilets above, and if that proved to be too shallow the cold tap above could be left running until the occupant remembered the answer to the question he had just been asked.

As they crossed the lawn, Slonský found himself staring at the building and reflecting that there must be many buildings around with a tale to tell every bit as horrible as the Red House's.

'There you are,' said Hanuš, pointing to the three flower beds in a row.

There was no doubt about it, the middle one of the three had a higher hump than the others, and assuming that they started level — and why would they not? — the obvious conclusion was that there was something under the soil that had not been there when Hanuš dug it over.

Slonský took his coat and jacket off and laid them on the lawn. 'Got a spare shovel?' he asked.

The first thing Hanuš observed was that the bed had been dug down deeper than he had gone. It was not a matter of something being placed in the bed as he had left it, because the dislodged earth went down more than two spades' depths. Something told Slonský they needed to work more slowly once this became clear, for fear that they might disturb some valuable evidence. He suggested to Hanuš that they should dig at the ends and then rake the loose soil to the edges for lifting out, thus avoiding digging downwards at the centre. It was not very long before the wisdom of this approach was demonstrated.

Hanuš felt something under his spade and was careful not to put any weight on it. Casting the tool to one side, he knelt down and clawed the soil away with his hands, and in no time at all they could see what had pushed the soil up.

'I think we'd better stop there and send for Dr Novák,' Slonský announced. 'He'll go ape if we interfere with his crime scene.'

'Well?' said Slonský.

'It's a woman,' said Dr Novák.

'I guessed that,' Slonský replied. 'The bright red nail polish put me onto it.'

'See? You're not a detective for nothing.'

'Cause of death?'

'She stopped breathing.'

'And why might that have happened, do you think?'

'Probably has something to do with that red line round her throat, but you tell me. I'm just the pathologist.'

'Strangled or garrotted?'

'Yes.'

'Which?'

'Don't know for sure yet, but probably strangled.'

'Has she been interfered with?' Slonský asked.

'No. No sign of sexual activity as such.'

'What do you mean, "as such"?'

'I mean there's no sign of anything being inserted anywhere, but maybe she was hoping, because that's pretty flimsy underwear to be walking around in. She's dressed for a date, I'd say. She had been wearing quite a smart suit. Probably cream when she put it on, though lying in soil hasn't helped its appearance.'

'Age?'

'Forties, maybe fifty. Not in the first flush of youth, shall we say, but nicely kept.'

'Wedding ring?'

'No. Nor any sign of one having been removed.'

'Shoes?'

'Shoes and handbag are missing.'

'How did she get here?'

'I doubt she walked, if that's what you're asking.'

Slonský winced. He had been trying to think how you would get a body over that wall which must be about one and a half metres tall, if not more. 'No sign of a car on the path or lawn, so she wasn't driven to her grave,' he said.

'No,' agreed Novák. 'But there are plenty of wheelbarrows around the grounds.'

'Time of death?'

'Just after she stopped breathing. Honestly, Slonský, I'll tell you as soon as I can but it's not straightforward. There's a complication.'

'What sort of complication?'

'I think she's been in a freezer.'

Slonský removed his hat and gave his head a good scratch before deciding it was too cold not to have a hat on and hastily replacing it. 'Why do you say that?'

'Because it's true. I'll know better when I've looked at some tissue samples, but there's still some ice in the folds of her clothes. Needless to say, that's going to make it difficult to pinpoint the time of death.'

'If Hanuš is right and the body was buried over the weekend, it's been here less than forty-eight hours.'

'Then your best guess at time of death is going to be based on when she was last seen alive, rather than anything I can tell you.'

'Why would you put a body in the freezer and then bury it?' Slonský asked.

'That's a question for a psychiatrist rather than a poor run of the mill pathologist.'

'I wouldn't describe you as run of the mill.'

'No?' said Novák hopefully.

'No. I'm far too polite.'

Novák smiled. Despite himself, he enjoyed his verbal sparring with Slonský, who was one of the few officers who ever said thank you and who completely trusted the professionalism of his work. Slonský just wouldn't admit it, that's all. Novák stood up and arched his back to allow himself to stand up straight after having been hunched over for a while. 'We'll take her back to the mortuary and I'll get to work. I'll be as quick as I can.'

'I appreciate that,' Slonský began. 'I realise you're probab— what is it?'

Novák had obviously seen something in the makeshift grave that puzzled, intrigued or concerned him and was walking slowly round the grave to see it from various angles. 'Slonský,' he said, 'would you do me a big favour?'

'Anything I can.'

'Good. Push off and annoy someone else for half an hour. If I'm right, I may have something very interesting for you, but I need to think long and hard first.'

'Your wish is my command. Half an hour?'

'Thereabouts.'

Slonský spotted Hanuš in the background and walked over to ask the key question of the morning. 'Anywhere nearby that does a good coffee?'

Slonský was leaning against the gatepost when Novák found him.

'Nice to see some people have time for coffee,' the pathologist remarked.

'I'd have brought you one, but it looked like you were busy.'

'I was, and so will you be in a minute. Come and see what I've found.'

Slonský's curiosity was piqued but it would not do to show it, so he affected an air of nonchalance as he strolled behind Novák.

'It would be a good idea if you resisted any temptation to jump into the grave and stamp all over the evidence in your size forty-fours,' Novák said.

'How do you know I take a size forty-four shoe?'

'I've told you before, I'm a world authority on footprints.'

'So you have. But I thought you were kidding.'

Novák scowled, as would any man who had just been asked to contribute a chapter on footprints to an international forensic encyclopaedia. 'You'll recall,' he said, 'that Hanuš told us he dug down a certain distance to turn over the top layer of soil.'

'Yes, my memory isn't that bad. It's only been an hour or so.'

'Then he noticed that someone had dug deeper,' Novák continued. 'Averaged out, they've gone down about sixty centimetres or so.'

'Right.'

'Then we hit compacted soil that hasn't been disturbed.'

'Except for a body being laid on it, yes.'

'Now, Slonský, here's the bit you'll find interesting.'

'I doubt that very much, but pray continue.'

Novák took his glasses off and polished them vigorously before continuing. Two of them could play that game of being extremely irritating, and he was not about to be bettered by Slonský. 'We've taken the body out and laid it beside the grave for easy comparison. Now, what do you notice?'

Slonský stepped back to get a better view, then squatted on his haunches. 'Is this a trick question?'

'Of course not. I don't do that.'

'The dent is too big,' decided Slonský.

'Correct. So what do we conclude?'

'She has shrunk since she's been dead?'

Novák sighed deeply. 'Not by six and a half centimetres. Not to mention having dropped around twenty kilos in weight.'

Slonský decided to start by eliminating the least likely answer. 'Dehydration?' he suggested.

'Dehydration? She's dead, man! Dead people don't drink.'

'That's a good reason for not being dead, then,' Slonský replied. 'I could do with a beer myself.'

'The impression in the earth was made by a different body,' Novák told him, speaking slowly as if addressing the dimmest student he had ever had.

'A different body? Well, where's it gone, then?'

'That's your job. My job is to tell you there was one, and your job is to find it. It's called demarcation.'

'It's called bloody weird, that's what it is. So someone else was buried here, then someone came along with a body, dug a hole, thought "Goodness me, this grave is already occupied but I'm not digging another damn hole, so I'll yank that one out and plant my one", and carted the first body off somewhere else.'

'That sounds a remarkably improbable reconstruction of the facts, Slonský, even by your standards.'

'To be honest, I can't think of any reconstruction of the facts that would be any more plausible.'

'Let me give you another clue. I've taken soil samples which I'll have to analyse, but my first impression is that the original body had been here quite some time.'

'How can you say that when it isn't here?'

'Because it's stained the soil in a characteristic way. Bones aren't forever, Slonský. They can deteriorate during life, but they can carry on doing so after you're dead. That's especially true if people are laid in shallow graves that are alternately wet and dry. I'm going to guess that this whole area was watered by the gardeners from time to time. Each time the soil gets wet, water seeps into the bones and washes minerals out. Those minerals dribble into the soil. If it goes on long enough you can be left with just a soil silhouette, a shape in the earth where the skeleton was. I don't think that one went this far, but it suffered some deterioration.'

'How long was it here?'

'It's very hard to say, but it's going to be years.'

Slonský decided that he needed a good scratch of the back of his thigh in order to process this information. 'So you're saying we've probably got two murders, one of which involves a body we haven't got who was killed a long time ago?'

'That's about the sum of it. Should be easy meat for a man of your ability, Slonský.'

'Don't mock me or there'll be a third corpse in this grave.'

'There's one piece of good news.'

'Is there? What is it?'

'It's almost impossible for an amateur working quickly to retrieve a whole body. While you're having lunch, we'll still be here going through that spoil heap looking for any tiny fragments of bone. I'll be surprised if we don't find any of the original occupant. And if we do, we'll be able to do some tests that, with any luck, will tell you the sex of the corpse and maybe even its age. But don't hold me to that.'

'There's no point. You'd just deny you ever said it was possible.'

Chapter 3

Slonský returned to his office and surveyed his empire from the rarefied heights of his new office chair. He had detected a crack in the frame of his old one, undoubtedly the result of inferior workmanship and nothing to do with the kilos he had put back on since becoming a captain, and had asked about a new chair, being both surprised and delighted to discover that as a captain he qualified for a chair with five castors and a little lever on the side that moved him up or down.

Having had it for a few days, during which he had twice involuntarily launched himself into the filing cabinet with sudden movements, he gave it to his assistant, Lieutenant Kristýna Peiperová, and switched back to an old-style chair, which had in turn come apart at a joint. The supplies people then came up with a magnificent high-backed chair like the throne of the potentate of a small country. It was not new, admittedly, but it had stood the test of time, and with a cushion at the back it was very comfortable.

Having cautioned Peiperová that the chair had a mind of its own and to exercise due care in its use, Slonský was surprised to discover that she sustained no injuries from it, but appeared to be able to control it perfectly well. If she wanted to turn, it turned; if she chose to roll to one side, she rolled just far enough. He attributed this to the lower centre of gravity of women which meant that they were very stable around the hips.

The new lieutenant, Peiperová, was doing well. Returned from an unhappy period as Personal Assistant to Colonel Urban, then the Director of Criminal Police and now Great

Lord Bigwig of Czech Policing overall, she had soon fitted right back in and was showing how right Slonský had been when he had pushed for her promotion.

The desk at the back of the room was newly occupied by Lucie Jerneková. She was still in uniform, having just completed six months' basic training after Slonský recruited her, having been impressed by her aggression, her observational powers and her unwillingness to take a backward step whatever life threw at her. He had cut a deal with Colonel Urban under which all Lucie's rotations after her first six months would be performed in his team, following which she would be appointed a trainee detective. For now she was just Officer Jerneková, trying to curb her tongue and grateful that she had a barracks to live in and some money in her purse. She was a little older than Peiperová but did not resent having been assigned to work under her, largely because she was completely indifferent to ranks. Although Czechs are generally quite informal people, she was the only person who routinely referred to all her colleagues, except Captain Slonský, by their first names.

The only colleague who found difficulty in reciprocating was Lieutenant Jan Navrátil, who was meticulous about the use of titles. During working hours, he even referred to his fiancée as Lieutenant Peiperová. Given that context, he could hardly refer to Officer Jerneková as Lucie.

Navrátil was a law graduate who had been fast-tracked at the Police Academy and then sent for detective training under the then Lieutenant Slonský. Slonský much preferred working on his own and would have refused had it not been that Captain Lukas had a nuclear option that he was prepared to deploy if necessary. At the time Slonský was coming up to retirement age; officers can only continue beyond that age with the agreement of their superiors, and Lukas let it be known that his agreement might be contingent on Slonský's willingness to take on a trainee. Since Slonský dreaded retirement, he had gritted his teeth and agreed. And in the event he had enjoyed it. Navrátil was young, idealistic, intelligent and hard-working. Slonský could only legitimately claim to score one out of four on that list. Even his idealism was tempered with some cynicism, though he retained hope that once his generation was out of the way people like Navrátil and Peiperová would make the police service what it was meant to be. He genuinely believed that Navrátil could one day be the Director of Police — if Peiperová didn't beat him to it.

Then there was the other recent arrival, Officer Ivo Krob. Krob had spent some years as a policeman in the Municipal Police in Prague. As a result, he was very pleased to have a job that was not usually conducted outdoors, though Slonský had noticed that it didn't worry Krob if they had to knock on doors in sub-zero temperatures or driving rain.

The chief characteristics of Krob were his relentless cheerfulness and his absolute faith in his boss. At first Slonský was very touched as Krob reassured victims of crime that Captain Slonský would sort things out for them, that Captain Slonský would soon be on top of their case, and that Captain Slonský had a knowledge of the city's criminals second to none; then it dawned on him that this one-man publicity machine was putting pressure on him to achieve superhuman results, so he had to ask Krob to remember this was a team effort and that it was the team that would succeed. Or not.

Krob was also very relaxed. Navrátil could become frustrated, and an explosion was never far away when Jerneková was having a bad day, but Krob just shrugged and got a coffee, then started again. He had a winning way with people, which was what had first brought him to Slonský's attention, and his other defining feature was his averageness. Krob was so average that Slonský had joked that it wouldn't surprise him to find that Krob had exactly 1.5 children. When he discovered that Krob actually had one child with another on the way, he trumpeted the fact that he was right, provided it was a ten-month pregnancy, since Mrs Krobová was five months gone at that point.

Slonský had resisted the reallocation of space that saw him separated from Navrátil and Peiperová and installed in Lukas' old office, but had come to realise that since their old room could not accommodate five, he would have had to choose to sit with either Navrátil and Krob, or Peiperová and Jerneková, and whichever choice he made might upset someone. Instead, he left his office door open and wandered back and forth as he saw fit; or, more often, bellowed for someone to come to him. Navrátil usually responded with alacrity, whereas Peiperová was more likely to call him on the internal phone to see what he wanted. Someday he must learn how to do that, he thought, but not today.

Slonský called the four of them into his office and filled them in on Novák's findings.

'Someone has taken the other body away?' repeated Navrátil.

'So I said,' Slonský replied.

'Why?' Navrátil asked.

'I don't know. Maybe you get cash back on bodies at the funeral home.'

'Did they know it was there, sir?' asked Peiperová.

'Ah, as usual you ask the key question, young lady. If they didn't, it must have come as a heck of a surprise.'

23

'But how would they know if the gardener didn't?' Peiperová persisted. 'Hasn't he dug it all over before?'

'No, lass, not all of it. That part of the garden was lawn until a year or so ago.'

'Presumably it wasn't lawn when the body was buried though,' Krob suggested, 'so if we could find when there was last a flower bed there, we might know when the person was killed.'

'Not quite so simple, unfortunately, though it's worth a try. The building was previously known as the Red House.'

'What's the Red House?' they chorused.

'That's the problem of employing you young people,' Slonský replied. 'You don't know so much. The Red House was an interrogation centre for the security services under Communism. People were taken there to be questioned, then either sent to court, given summary punishment or — rarely — sent home.'

'So this is one of those they executed?' Navrátil asked.

'I doubt it, if only because they usually executed them elsewhere, then they'd cremate the bodies and use the ashes to melt snow. We wouldn't have a body for most of those they executed. My guess is that this was someone who died during questioning, which doesn't mean that what happened there wasn't criminal, of course, just that they may not have deliberately killed him or her.'

'So this is pre-1989,' Krob continued.

'Certainly, unless the current security forces aren't telling us something. That's why you may not find any photographs in the archives. The StB weren't too keen for people to walk around the gardens of their places snapping the flowers. For that matter, you'd have to pay a photographer quite a bit extra before one would be prepared to try.'

'Will the files list the people who were arrested by the StB, sir?' Navrátil asked.

'Strangely, they might. Not as openly as we do it now, but there'll be daybooks and arrest records if they weren't hurriedly destroyed when the old regime fell. It's worth asking Mucha though. If a file exists, he's the person most likely to sniff it out.'

'Why are we more interested in the first one than the woman who has just been killed?' Jerneková demanded.

'We're not. We just don't yet have all the information that would help us to find out who she is. Once we get Novák's report we can try comparing her with any women reported missing, but in the meantime you can get a list of women between, say, thirty and sixty so it's ready as soon as we need it.' Slonský stood up and looked around the table. 'Does everyone know what they're doing?'

'I think so,' said Navrátil.

'Good. We're probably the only team in the police force that can say that. Let's keep it that way.'

Slonský's own contribution was to decamp to a nearby bar where he expected to find his friend Valentin, a celebrated journalist whose scoops were nearly all provided by Slonský in exchange for the possibility of planting stories in the press that suited Slonský's immediate needs. A number of senior officers had found their inadequacies and errors paraded before the public in the pages of Valentin's paper over the years.

'You're early,' Valentin remarked.

'So are you,' Slonský countered.

'No, I usually get here about now. The bar isn't too busy in the afternoon, so it's a good place to write my stories. I can't cope with all the noise in the newspaper office.'

'Yes, I suppose all that activity must be very off-putting.'

'You don't seem your usual bouncy self, Josef.'

'I'm not. The weirdest thing has happened. We've found a body.'

'I could be wrong, but I think that's happened before,' Valentin remarked.

'This one is different. This one is in a makeshift grave that was previously occupied by another murder victim. And the first victim has been removed.'

'Isn't stealing a corpse illegal or something?'

'Yes, but I don't think that's going to worry the guy too much when we charge him with murdering a woman.'

'Which woman?' Valentin asked.

'I don't know,' Slonský replied. 'Unidentified at present.'

'And who was the first victim?'

'Weren't you listening? He's not there, so we don't know.'

'Oh. I thought you went to dig up the first one and found the second one.'

'No, neither was properly buried.'

Valentin knocked back a small schnapps. 'It's going to make your job a lot more difficult if criminals start taking away the bodies of people killed by other criminals,' he said. 'So where is he going to bury the spare corpse he's now got? Why not just leave it where it was?'

'They wouldn't both fit.'

'Couldn't he dig a bigger hole?'

'And what would he do with the soil?'

'Well, it's got to be easier to get rid of some soil than a second-hand stiff.'

Slonský's signal had finally been spotted by a waiter and a beer arrived in front of him. 'That's a good point though,' he said. 'What's he going to do with that other body? He can't just put it in the freezer.'

'Why would he do that?' Valentin asked.

'That's where he kept the other one.'

Valentin was completely confused. 'He put a body in the freezer. Why?'

'To stop it going off, I suppose.'

'Why take it home? You can't simply plonk it on the sofa. It'll take a hell of a lot of explaining when you have visitors.'

'These are all good questions, old friend,' Slonský replied, 'I just don't have good answers.'

'And where was all this?'

Slonský lowered his voice. 'The Red House.'

'Jesus Maria! You've been in there? What were you thinking of?'

'The body was in the garden. Anyway, it's a teacher training college now.'

'Yes, they used to pretend their buildings had benign purposes. Didn't it occur to you that if there's a body in the grounds of the Red House there's no great mystery about who killed him? And if they buried him there, they didn't want anyone asking any questions about him?'

'Whoever he is — or she is — they're entitled to have their killing investigated. Whatever happened to the fearless reporter?' Slonský asked.

'He disappeared once other fearless reporters of his own age started getting banged up,' Valentin replied.

'I don't suppose there's anything in your files about the Red House?'

'Certainly not! And if I find anything, I'll burn it.'

'It was closed nearly twenty years ago. Those days are gone now.'

27

'Yes, Josef, but those people who worked there aren't, and they still know all those clever little tricks with lighted matches under your fingernails and steel wool on your scrotum.'

'You aren't cowed, are you?'

'Are you serious? Of course I am. And so should you be. The people who ran the Red House were among the most sadistic bastards this country has ever produced.'

'They'll be old men now,' Slonský said dismissively.

'Right. So they'll be grumpy old sadistic bastards. They're the worst kind. Be very, very careful, Josef. These fellows can be dangerous.'

Chapter 4

Novák had managed to deduce a few extra snippets from information from his examination of the corpse. The woman stood 164cm tall, had naturally light brown hair that had been tinted blonde, pale blue-grey eyes, did not appear to have had children, and was probably at or around the menopause, given the density of her bones. She had a small scar above her left eyebrow and Novák thought she probably wore spectacles most of the time though there were none with the body. And it seemed that her body had been wrapped in a dark red or maroon carpet or rug.

'Is that all?' said Slonský.

Novák replied by putting the phone down.

A few minutes later, the fax machine delivered Slonský a photograph of the body with a note that Novák had sent it to the police artist to have a version made with the eyes open.

Jerneková took the details Novák had provided and compared them with those of the women known to be missing. She did not have photographs for all of them, but it was soon clear that there were only four who were about the right size, colouring and age. A quick glimpse at a photograph ruled out one, whose face shape was wrong. There were no images for two, and the fourth had only been reported missing that morning and had been seen on Saturday, so it seemed very unlikely that she could have been killed, put in a freezer and buried in time to be found on Tuesday, particularly since the burial must have taken place on Saturday or Sunday.

'Right,' said Slonský, 'get yourself over to the people who reported the women missing and show them this photograph. I know her eyes are closed, but they can at least tell you if it's definitely not her.' Too late, he remembered the new chain of command. 'If that's all right with Lieutenant Peiperová,' he quickly added.

'You're in charge,' said Peiperová amicably.

'Why?' asked Slonský. 'Has something gone wrong?'

There was a ritual that had developed over the years that Navrátil had learned could not be varied. When Dr Novák said he had some findings, Slonský went to him, and not the other way around; and if Slonský went to Novák, he usually expected Navrátil to go too, partly because it provided him with a driver.

In the twenty-six months that Navrátil had worked for Slonský — after the first couple of days — there had never been any misunderstanding about their roles. While Slonský was entitled to a police car, and held a driving licence (albeit one arranged by the Army after he attended tank-driving school), he detested driving in Prague and was very happy to get someone else to drive him around. That was usually Navrátil or Peiperová. Slonský had yet to experience Krob's driving, and fortunately for Krob he had not suffered Slonský's either. Jerneková did not drive, but her name had been put down for driving lessons at the police school.

Slonský would drive on the major roads or anywhere outside Prague, maintaining a steady five kilometres an hour over whatever the speed limit currently was, but even then he would look to hand over the wheel when he felt peckish so that he could use both hands for coffee and a pastry. Peiperová had once woken from a nap on a long journey to discover Slonský with a coffee in one hand and a párek in the other, managing the steering wheel with his two smallest fingers and a knee, and after that she had been quick to volunteer to drive.

Novák's phone call summoned Slonský, who grabbed his hat and coat and beckoned Navrátil to come with him. For many trips around Prague public transport was quicker, but since there were parking spaces outside the mortuary Navrátil collected a car and soon they pulled up outside the building and trotted up the steps to the familiar doors.

Novák was in his office, clad in an immaculate white coat with an impressive selection of ballpoint pens in his breast pocket. He invited his guests to sit and blinked at them a couple of times through the thick lenses of his glasses before reaching for a small transparent plastic box which he slid across the desktop until it rested in front of Slonský.

'A finger bone, probably the right ring finger's lowest section. It belonged to a man, and that's about all we can say for certain. My best guess is that it had been in the ground there for twenty years or more, but it's hard to be definite and I wouldn't swear to that in court.'

'Age at death?'

'A mature man, so let's say older than twenty-five, and no arthritic changes at the top surface, though if there were they might not have survived anyway.'

'Height?'

'She was 164. He was around six or seven centimetres taller. I'm not going to try to project a person's height from a single finger bone.'

Navrátil rarely asked questions of Novák, preferring to leave it to Slonský, but now that he had progressed to the rank of lieutenant he felt empowered to ask his own. 'Does it surprise you that you only found one bone?' he asked.

'Frankly, yes,' Novák replied. 'Someone working after dark, as they must have done, without anything more than a lantern or flashlight, must have been very careful indeed to collect all the material.'

'Perhaps only one bone was buried in the first place,' Slonský suggested.

'Who would only bury one bone?' asked Novák.

'Bobík.'

'Bobík? Who is Bobík?'

'My childhood dog,' Slonský replied. 'Never buried two bones in the same place. I suppose it's some sort of risk management strategy for dogs.'

'Slonský, neither of the bodies were buried by a dog,' Novák said. 'In fact, the woman was buried by a fairly strong individual. She was around fifty-eight kilos in weight.'

'That brings us back to the question of how the killer got her over the wall,' Slonský commented. 'And the only way to determine that is to go to the Red House again and heave a body over the wall. Navrátil, how much do you weigh?'

Having ascertained that Navrátil tipped the scales at around sixty-four kilos, Slonský was attempting to lift him over the wall, to the amusement of those passing by on the lane that ran down the side of the Red House's south wall.

'There must have been two of them,' Slonský decided. 'Even with your co-operation I can't get you up that high. Are you sure you're only sixty-four kilos, lad?'

'Last time I weighed myself, sir. Of course, I'd just come out of the shower.'

'Unless you've got unusually heavy underwear that wouldn't make much of a difference.'

Navrátil was jumping up and down on the spot.

'What are you doing, Navrátil?'

'Trying to see the grave, sir.'

'Why don't we just walk round and look at it?'

'I'm wondering how he would know where to put her over the wall. It's not necessarily the case that she went over at the point nearest to the grave.'

Slonský scratched his chin in thought. 'That's true.' He looked along the length of the wall. 'But there's nowhere substantially lower, is there?'

'No, sir, but perhaps there's a place where he would be less conspicuous to passers-by.'

They strolled along the wall. At one point there were bushes against the wall, which militated against getting close enough to pass a corpse over it, but Slonský suddenly stopped and pointed upwards. 'When we get inside, let's see what's behind those trees, shall we?'

If Navrátil was unaffected by walking through the gates, the same could hardly be said of Slonský, who felt a shiver as he crossed the boundary.

'It looks so ordinary,' Navrátil remarked.

'Evil often does,' Slonský replied. 'If you look at a gallery of serial killers they resemble people you'd meet in a post office.'

The burial site was still roped off with incident tape, so Navrátil could see which way to go and strode to the flower bed.

'When you arrived, sir, was the whole flower bed disturbed?'

'Good question. No, when you stand with your back to the wall, the left end was slightly higher than the right.'

'Then how did the killer know where to dig?' Navrátil asked.

'Explain yourself,' said Slonský, though he was beginning to understand a little better himself.

'Well, the killer arrives with body number two. But he didn't just come across body number one, did he? If it was a surprise to him there was no reason to take it away. He could either leave body two here anyway or, if he wanted to avoid detection, he takes it somewhere else. It's a nuisance for him, but either way he leaves body one. What point is there in taking it away unless he always intended to do that?'

'If Novák is right,' Slonský replied, 'and he usually is, then the murderer invested a lot of time in collecting a set of bones and taking them away. And while a red carpet may have been fine for bringing an intact body here, it wouldn't be much help in taking a disconnected skeleton away, so we have to assume that he came with some kind of holdall or sack.'

'In which event he came prepared, and we can deduce that he knew that there was a body here,' Navrátil said.

'That puts a different complexion on things, doesn't it? For a start, how did he know that?'

'And how did he know where it was, given that the gardener didn't? He didn't have to dig the entire bed up.' Navrátil paced the length of the bed. 'This must be about five metres, sir, but he picks the correct two metres to dig up.'

'Not so fast, lad. He may have started in the middle and extended in the direction he needed to go once he found something.'

'Perhaps. But either way, he knew there was a body under this flower bed.'

Slonský glanced around in each direction. 'I can't see any obvious markers or alignments.'

'Go back twenty or thirty years, sir. You've had a prisoner die under questioning and you need to dispose of the body. What would make you put it here? Why not right at the back?'

'There must have been something here that made it a good pick. Nowadays it's too open. You'd see that the ground had been dug up.'

Navrátil had walked back to the main driveway and was counting steps again.

'What is it, lad?'

'The path forks north and south, but the south fork is shorter than the north one. You see, sir, it's closer to the building. I bet it wasn't built that way.'

'It would have been symmetrical at the outset. Obviously that little wing that juts out on the north-east side wasn't there then, but otherwise it looks like two identical sides to the building, north and south.'

'Yes, sir, but why put the main door here, in the west side, and then put the lawn to the right? Wouldn't the building be in the middle of the site? And wouldn't the main lawn be in front of the main door?'

'I'm not an architect, Navrátil. Those fellows have some funny ideas.'

'It would be good to know what was here before.'

'There's absolutely no chance that the StB will have produced a guidebook. I'll be surprised if we can find a photograph from the last fifty years.'

'Maybe so, sir, but that wall isn't new, so a photograph before that might give us a clue.'

'You won't let it rest, will you?' Valentin sighed, as Slonský badgered him again.

'Valentin, are you going to look for a photo in your archives or do I have to send a couple of heavies in with a warrant?'

'Our editor wouldn't be frightened of that.'

'I could send Peiperová and Jerneková.'

'Now let's not be hasty. There's no need for that sort of threat.'

'You've never met Jerneková.'

'You said she was like a slightly more female version of the young you, and that's an awful enough image for me. I'll see what I can find.'

'Good. Drink up.'

'Drink up? Josef, it's not even half past seven.'

'No time like the present. We'll get a bottle of something warming to take with us. I imagine that your office can offer us a couple of glasses for the schnapps.'

'We're not complete savages, you know.'

Slonský tucked the schnapps in his coat pocket and they took the Metro to Valentin's newspaper's office.

'I'll have to get you past security somehow,' Valentin muttered.

'Security? Is this the usual muscle-bound goons in black t-shirts?'

'No, it's a couple of old soldiers who need a bit of pocket money.'

Slonský produced his badge and held it up for inspection.

'I don't want to be awkward…' began one of the guards.

'Then don't be,' Slonský responded. 'If any shooting starts, just keep down behind your desks. My men will keep you safe. But mum's the word, eh? Don't want to jeopardise a carefully planned police operation, do we?'

The two old soldiers agreed at once that they would not indulge in any heroics, would keep away from the windows and would not tell anyone Slonský was inside the building.

'Easy peasy,' muttered Slonský as he and Valentin climbed the stairs. 'No-one will ever know I was here.'

The office was surprisingly quiet given that a new issue was going to press in just a few hours.

'A lot of the journalists work from home and email their articles in these days,' Valentin explained.

'And you don't?'

'No, for two reasons. My typewriter doesn't do email, and I wouldn't work at home when I could be sitting in a nice warm bar.' Valentin pointed to an office where a light could be seen. 'That's a stroke of luck. The picture editor is in. Come on.'

Valentin effected introductions and explained that Captain Slonský was involved in a case that required him to look for old photographs of the Red House.

'I doubt we'd have any,' the picture editor argued. 'The StB were funny about that kind of thing.'

'Before their time,' Slonský explained. 'I want to know what it was like before they got their hands on it.'

'Well, our archives only go back to the end of the First World War,' the editor said, 'but we have access to some online libraries of photographs that go back further. What was it called before it became the Red House?'

'I don't know. It was the home of some baron or other.'

'Okay, let's start there. I'll bring up a map of Prague and you can show me where exactly it is.'

Slonský soon located it, and the editor, who had introduced himself as Matěj, then found a map of Prague in 1908 so that they could compare the modern and antique versions.

'There we are,' said Matěj. 'It's described as the home of the Baron Pfarrenstein. I've heard of him. He was a minor Austrian baron who married the daughter of a Czech noble and came here because that's where his wife's money was. He was small fry in Vienna but a big fish in Prague.'

Matěj found a photograph of Pfarrenstein and displayed it on his monitor. A small, tubby man with a black spade-shaped beard and pince-nez, his coat was embellished with a number of insignia and medals and he wore a sash over his waistcoat.

'There are fifteen photographs in this particular library of the house,' Matěj announced, and displayed them as thumbnails on the screen. None showed anything other than the actual house. 'What about news stories about him and his house?' Slonský demanded.

Matěj typed a number of phrases into a search box and they waited impatiently as the computer totalled up the number of files it was scanning. Finally it declared itself finished and a list flashed up.

'That one,' said Slonský, pointing at one halfway down the page.

Matěj clicked on the heading and a poor quality clipping from a newspaper appeared. It showed a middle-aged man in waistcoat and shirt sleeves with a large chain across his midriff, a detachable collar on his shirt and a walrus moustache of gigantic proportions, holding his prize exhibit for the approbation of the reader.

'Now, where at the Red House could you grow a pineapple?' Slonský wondered aloud.

'There must have been hothouses,' Valentin answered.

'And they would have been on the south side to get maximum sun,' added Slonský.

Matěj tried a few more search terms, and was rewarded with exactly what Slonský had been looking for.

'That's why the path was moved nearer the building. They needed to accommodate that glasshouse. What is it — six metres north to south, and maybe half as long again east to west? Now, the next question is, when was it removed?' Slonský asked.

'I doubt that the computer will tell us that,' Matěj declared, 'but the answer may be elsewhere in the building.' He picked up his telephone and rang a number on the internal system, inviting the recipient of his call to come up to his office. A few minutes later there was a knock at the door and one of the security guards entered, swiftly removing his cap and tucking it under his arm.

'Jaroslav, you're a keen gardener, aren't you?' Matěj asked him.

'Like my father before me.'

'We've got a question and I'm hoping you may know where we can get the answer. We've got a cutting about a prize pineapple grown in a greenhouse in the garden of the house of Baron Pfarrenstein, the building that became known as the Red House. Any idea when the greenhouse was demolished?'

'It was still there when I was a young man,' said Jaroslav, stroking his cheek as if the action might coax some further memories to his brain.

'Can you be more precise?' Slonský asked him.

Jaroslav's eyes lit up as if some recollection had just come to him. 'It was there in 1968, because after the Russians invaded I can remember some students went to the Red House and lobbed stones over the walls to break the glass. It stayed like that for a while and then the authorities bulldozed it rather than go to the trouble of repairing it, because every time they replaced the glass someone would break it again.'

'So it was there until, what, 1969, 1970, 1971?'

'Something like that. Sooner rather than later. By the end of 1969 they'd got control back, and I don't think anyone in their right mind would have tried to break the glass again. Of course they hadn't grown anything there in years, what with what the Red House was used for. I suppose you know…' he began, but then his voice tailed away as if he could not bear to describe its use.

Valentin was the first to speak. 'So if you had a body to bury, a disused greenhouse might have been a really good place. You'd have the soil, and once the greenhouse was demolished the grass would have been allowed to cover it all.'

'That's right,' agreed Slonský, 'and while it's not conclusive on date, it gives us an idea about when it might have happened. It could have been before, and it could have been a little while after, before the lawn grew over the site, but it's a possible answer for one of our questions. If the killer knew the first body was buried in the greenhouse he'd have a start, but it's still a long site to excavate looking for it.'

'It wouldn't be that difficult,' Jaroslav answered. 'Most of the greenhouse was usually given over to pots and trestles with plants sitting on top. The only part where ground-level soil was used was right in the middle.'

'And how would you fix the middle?' Slonský demanded to know.

Jaroslav had a suggestion. 'My father told me that back when he was a boy, an airship flew over Prague and took some photographs. The glasshouse was big enough to show up on those.'

Matěj hurriedly searched his database once more. 'Bingo! Aerial views of Prague, 1930. And there's the Pfarrenstein mansion.'

'And the door of the greenhouse is opposite the third bay window. That's how our man knew where the body would be. He must have heard all this somehow,' Slonský said. 'But how?'

Chapter 5

Jerneková had drawn a blank with the last pair of missing persons, neither of whom was the woman in the flower bed, as she was described in the evening paper. Slonský was annoyed that the story had leaked out. If there was any leaking to be done, he wanted to do it, and Valentin was his vessel of choice, but then he reflected that he had planned to put the photograph in the newspaper anyway, and it was only the fact of the death and the location of the body that he had intended to suppress for now. Unusually, the publication in the evening newspaper brought immediate results when a woman telephoned to say that she thought she might recognise the person in the picture.

Peiperová and Jerneková were dispatched to speak to her.

Eva Čechová was a woman in her late twenties who worked for the university in one of its administrative departments. She had telephoned from work and was waiting for the two police officers in the foyer of the grand building that housed her office when they arrived. They sat on one of the benches there.

'You think you recognise the woman in the photograph?' began Peiperová.

'I think so,' Eva replied. 'It looks like Adalheid Rezeková who works in the student registry with me.'

'When did you last see her?' Peiperová continued.

'About ten days ago. The registry staff are restricted on when we can take our holidays because our busy times are during the university vacations, so we take ours during the semesters. I wasn't expecting to see Adalheid last week because she had booked a few days off, but when she didn't return on Monday as expected I began to worry.'

'Does she have family?'

'Her parents are still alive, but I don't know that she ever mentioned anyone else. She was a very private person.'

'Do you know where she lives?'

'I'm afraid not. But our human resources department would. They have all our home addresses.'

'I'll ask them once we know that she is definitely missing,' said Peiperová with an encouraging smile. 'I have another photograph of her, but I have to warn you that it was taken after her death.'

'That's okay,' Eva gulped.

Peiperová glanced around to ensure that nobody was looking over their shoulders, then opened her bag and produced the post-mortem image.

'I think that's her,' Eva confirmed. 'I never saw her with her hair down like that and she usually wore glasses, but the face shape is right. What happened to her?'

'I'm afraid she was murdered.'

Eva gasped and held her hand over her mouth for a moment.

'Did she have a partner or boyfriend?' Peiperová enquired.

'She was divorced,' Eva replied. 'It was a long time ago and it didn't last long. I think it was straight after she left university. I don't know that she had a regular long-term boyfriend. If we had any social events she usually came alone, if she bothered at all. But she had met someone lately. I'm not sure it was exactly romantic, but she remarked that she had been invited out to dinner by a man recently.'

'How recently?' Peiperová asked.

'Just before the holiday. She was meeting him on the Wednesday or Thursday. But I've seen her since then.'

'Did she say how it went?' Jerneková wanted to know.

'She said it was interesting. She wasn't gushy about it, but then she never was. I think she was quite hurt by her marriage and she was fairly cynical about her chances of finding happiness. But I think she still hoped, deep down. Don't we all?'

'No,' said Jerneková firmly.

Peiperová glowered at Jerneková, who remained blissfully unaware of her boss's displeasure.

'Perhaps we could all go to the human resources department. They may have a photograph on file and we can ask about her address too.' Eva led the way and explained the request to the woman on the desk, who took no time at all to decide that this was something well beyond her pay grade, so she fetched one of the managers.

'You're asking for personal information about one of our staff?' he said.

Peiperová produced her own identification. 'First, we want to see if you have a photograph of a woman who worked here who may have been murdered. I assume there's no objection to helping us to confirm the identity of a victim?'

'No, I suppose not.'

'I'm sure if she was lying unconscious in hospital having been hit by a car you'd want to help,' Jerneková added, with just a hint that this was precisely the kind of accident that might befall someone who decided not to co-operate with their enquiry.

'Oh, quite,' he agreed.

'I think it's Adalheid Rezeková,' Eva explained.

'Rezeková, Adalheid,' the man said as he wrote it down before adding a completely unnecessary 'wait here' as he turned to walk away. After a few minutes he returned with a folder and an index card. 'That's Ms Rezeková,' he said.

'There's certainly a strong likeness,' agreed Peiperová, offering him the post-mortem photograph so he could see for himself.

'Oh, my goodness!' he exclaimed. 'Has she been strangled?'

'Probably,' Jerneková confirmed. 'Perhaps garrotted. Either way, done to death nastily.'

'Do you have her address?' asked Peiperová.

The manager, now thoroughly flustered, searched ineffectively for it until Jerneková plonked her stubby finger on the top right hand corner of the folder itself.

'That looks like an address.'

'Yes, indeed, that's where it would be,' he agreed. 'I'm sorry, I'm not as used to violent death as you obviously are.'

'I don't suppose you would be,' agreed Jerneková, glossing over the fact that this was the first murder case that she had been involved in and copying the address into her notebook.

'What about a next of kin? Do you keep notes of that?' Peiperová asked.

'Oh, certainly, in case of sickness or accidents.' The manager rustled through the pages, then thought to look on the front cover again. 'Here we are.'

Peiperová read the entry and felt a little queasy. The man described as Rezeková's father was General Klement Rezek (retired).

In the car on the way to the General's house, Peiperová suggested to Jerneková that it would be good if she let Peiperová do most of the talking, given the delicate nature of their duty and the fact that the General and his wife were likely to be very elderly.

'I'm not completely insensitive, you know,' Jerneková protested, to which response Peiperová allowed herself to raise an eyebrow. 'I'm not! And I've been trained to break bad news. But it won't do me any harm to see how you do it,' Jerneková conceded.

General Rezek and his wife lived in a large single-storey villa in the northern outskirts of Prague. There was a substantial garden, partly given over to growing vegetables, but there was also a post in the centre where an aggressive black dog was barking loudly and straining at a substantial chain attached to his collar.

'I don't think I'll pet that one,' Jerneková muttered.

'I hope that's not a portent of his owner,' Peiperová replied.

They reached the door without mishap and rang the bell. It was opened by a stocky man with a stiff brush of steel-coloured hair. He was wearing a heavy workman's shirt with the sleeves turned back to reveal a thickly-muscled pair of forearms.

The officers identified themselves and confirmed that they were speaking to General Rezek. It seemed unthinkable not to use his rank, although he had clearly been retired for twenty years or more.

Rezek stood in the doorway and showed no sign of inviting them in.

'I wonder if we might step inside a moment,' Peiperová asked. 'Our duty is a delicate one.'

Without a word, he stepped back and they were able to enter the hallway.

'I'm afraid we have some bad news for you,' Peiperová told him. 'We have reason to believe that a woman who has been killed may be your daughter Adalheid.'

Rezek flinched momentarily, then recovered himself. 'And how did you identify her?'

'Colleagues of hers had reported her missing and have identified her from a photograph.'

Rezek held out his hand. 'Let me see.'

'I should warn you that it's a post-mortem photograph.'

Rezek gestured impatiently for Peiperová to hand the photograph over, took it in his hand and glanced at it. Without a word, he handed it back.

'Is that Adalheid?' Peiperová asked.

'Yes.'

'We have to ask you to formally identify her body, I'm afraid.'

Rezek raised his chin defiantly. 'Of course. But first I must tell my wife what has happened. Please sit in there while I do so.'

He held open a door and ushered the two officers through. The room into which they were shown was dominated by a large portrait of Rezek in his military uniform.

'How did he manage to stay upright with all those medals hanging off his chest?' Jerneková whispered.

'I think they stiffened the uniform, otherwise the cloth would tear,' Peiperová replied.

'He looks fierce.'

'That's how he wanted us to see him. Now he's just an old man who has lost his daughter.'

Through the other door to the room, Peiperová could see Rezek with an arm round his wife's shoulders as she wiped her face on her apron. There was the sound of subdued sobbing but Mrs Rezeková remained in the kitchen, unable or unwilling to speak to the police officers.

Rezek collected his jacket and reappeared behind them. 'Let's go,' he said, with the air of a man who expected his decisions to be final.

At the mortuary, Rezek said barely a word. He greeted Dr Novák formally, followed him to the room where Adalheid had been placed, and stood stiffly as the sheet was drawn back from the face.

'That is my daughter Adalheid,' he said without obvious emotion before stepping forward and kissing her on the forehead.

Novák and the officers offered their condolences, which Rezek acknowledged with a nod of his head before stepping back a pace or so to stand to attention. After a while, he dipped his head in salute and turned to leave the room.

'Who is in charge of the investigation?' he asked. 'I'd like to speak to him.'

If Lieutenant Peiperová was at all disconcerted by Rezek's assumption that a young woman could not possibly be leading a murder inquiry, she hid it well. Jerneková was finding it rather more difficult but kept silent until they had delivered Rezek to Slonský's office.

Peiperová explained to Slonský that they had identified the dead woman as General Rezek's daughter Adalheid. Slonský invited the General to sit and expressed his sympathy for his loss.

'I assume you will be putting your best man on this case,' Rezek said. There may not have been any emphasis on the word "man", but it was fairly clear that in his mind the best "man" could not possibly be a woman, or, at least, not one as young as the two in front of him.

'I superintend all the work we do,' Slonský replied, 'and my whole team will be involved. Lieutenant Peiperová and Officer Jerneková have my full confidence, and I'm sure that they will earn yours too.'

Rezek chose not to press the matter any further. 'I assume you will have some questions for me,' he commented, without any interrogative tone at all in the remark.

'It would help if you could confirm her home address,' Slonský began.

The General produced a small card from his wallet with Adalheid's address and telephone number on it. They matched those given by the university.

'Thank you,' Slonský said, after copying the information onto his desk pad and circling it in red so he had a fair chance of finding it again later and remembering what it was. 'Was she married?'

'Divorced. She married young to an unsuitable man. It didn't last long.'

'Were they still in touch?'

'I doubt it. He's dead.'

'How did that happen?'

'Car crash. Probably drunk — he usually was.'

'When did that happen?'

Rezek counted on his fingers. 'She was forty-eight years old, and she married at twenty-three. It lasted about two years, and he died soon after the divorce.'

'So over twenty years ago?'

'About that.'

In other words, thought Slonský, *it was before the Wall came down.* 'Do you have other children?'

'A son, Petr. But he was by my first wife.'

'Whereas Adalheid was not?'

'Her mother married me nearly fifty years ago. Petr must be fifty-seven by now.'

'We should tell him what has happened to his sister. Do you have an address for him?'

'No. We don't talk. His choice.'

'That must be difficult.'

'Difficult or not, it's how things are. He's a journalist and ashamed of my service to my country, so he disowned me. He doesn't use my name, preferring to use his mother's. He works as Petr Vlk.'

The name rang a distant bell somewhere in Slonský's head, but he chose not to pursue it. 'Were you close to your daughter?'

'She was dutiful. She visited us regularly. We rarely come into the city these days. It's not congenial.'

By which you mean that you might meet someone who remembers you, Slonský decided. 'And she worked at the University.'

'Yes, for many years.'

'Did she have outside interests?'

'She read a lot, went to concerts. If you're asking if she had a gentleman friend, then I have no idea. She would not have told me, and I don't think she had that kind of relationship with her mother either.'

'I wasn't thinking particularly of that,' Slonský replied, 'but thank you anyway.'

'Where do you propose to start?' Rezek demanded.

'The forensic scientists will complete their report soon. Lieutenant Peiperová and Officer Jerneková will search her flat for any clues about her movements. You haven't asked me where her body was found.'

49

'If you wish me to know, no doubt you will tell me.'

'It's a place that might have a meaning for people of our generation. She was in the grounds of the Red House.' For just a moment there were clear signs in Rezek's face that this meant something to him. 'Can you think, General, of any reason why someone would go to a lot of trouble to leave her there?'

'No. I'm sure she would not have gone to such a place voluntarily.'

'But you are familiar with the building and its past use?'

'I'm not a child, Captain. You want to know if I have any connection with it. And you will no doubt have discovered that I was previously a General in the StB.'

Slonský had not, but this had saved him a bit of work in the files. Since the lines between the Army and the security police were blurred at the best of times, he had suspected that this might have been the case.

'And did you ever work in the Red House?' he asked.

'From time to time. We all did, when our cases demanded it. But I have not set foot in the place for nearly twenty years.'

Slonský stood to indicate that the interview was over. 'Thank you for your assistance, General. We will keep in touch. But now the ladies will drive you home so that you can be with your wife. We have specially trained support officers —'

'Thank you, that will not be necessary.'

Rezek shook Slonský's hand and strode from the room, paying no attention to the two women who were compelled to run behind him. Peiperová responded first, with Jerneková straggling behind because she had stayed to exchange a word or two with Slonský.

'Callous bastard, isn't he?' she said.

Chapter 6

Slonský could think of no better way to collect information on a journalist than to ask another journalist, and since Valentin was a creature of habit who spent most of the hours of daylight in one or other of the nearby bars, it took him only ten minutes to track him down.

'Petr Vlk?' Valentin asked. 'Of course I remember him. You must, too.'

'I don't.'

'Petr Vlk? Of course you do.'

'I say I don't,' Slonský repeated. 'Maybe I should, but I don't.'

'He was a high flyer about a generation ago. Used to front up that programme on television. His dad was something in the Army, I think.'

'I've met the dad. Ex-StB General. Nasty piece of work.'

'That'll be the one,' Valentin confirmed. 'Well, his son was much the same. Got somewhere on the back of Daddy's name. But he wasn't called Vlk then.'

'His dad is General Rezek,' Slonský told him.

'Rezek! That's it. He changed to Vlk when stories came out about what his dad had been up to. There was a spectacular falling out. The son thought he was bulletproof, but he forgot that Daddy giveth and Daddy can taketh away, so when he turned on his father publicly he got sacked by the state broadcaster.'

'Why is that not a surprise?'

'And since the standard of his work was even lower than theirs, he couldn't get a job for ages. He tried to attach himself to Havel and the Charter 77 mob, but they thought he was an agent provocateur planted by his father, so they never took him in. He finally managed to reinvent himself as a theatre and restaurant critic. This allows him to indulge his favourite hobby.'

'Which is?'

'Getting hammered at other people's expense. He's very good at it,' Valentin said admiringly.

'You're not too shabby yourself,' Slonský replied, calling the waiter over for a refill.

'I'm an amateur compared with him. For a start, I can hold my booze. By great good fortune, when I've had too much I just fall asleep. I'm no trouble to anyone.'

Slonský edged away from Valentin along the bench seat.

'What are you doing?' Valentin asked.

'Giving the Almighty a clearer target in case he decides to send down a thunderbolt. No trouble to anyone? What about the time you impersonated Tina Turner on the bar counter?'

'I don't remember that. Sure it was me?'

'Dead certain.'

'It doesn't sound like the sort of thing I'd do. For a start I can't sing.'

'A fact which soon became all too clear.'

Valentin shrugged. 'You live and learn. Anyway, Vlk is still writing the occasional column for one of our competitors. He also seems to have cornered the market in those giveaway magazines you see in tourist centres, where he recommends restaurants that meet his key criteria.'

'Which are?'

'A willingness to pay a suitable fee and keep him in free dinners.'

'That sounds like an expensive way to buy publicity.'

'They probably don't realise that when they sign up. So do you want to meet this Vlk character?' Valentin asked.

'I've got to tell him his sister has been killed.'

'That won't be fun. Shall I meet you here at seven o'clock?'

'I can't. I've got to find Vlk, remember?'

'That's what we're going to do. There's no point trying to find him before, because he doesn't get up until late afternoon.'

You had to hand it to Sergeant Mucha. If there was anyone in the Czech police service who knew where to find a file, he was the one. It was widely believed that when the Wall came down and everyone knew what was going to happen next, the StB had burned all the incriminating files. There was good evidence for this, because many people recalled the Little Bonfires, a period of about a fortnight during which the country's fire brigades were repeatedly called out to deal with fires in the middle of fields, many of which appeared to involve burning documents. It was true that the StB had started many fires and had burned a lot of documents, but it was barely scratching the surface. To Mucha's certain knowledge at least four million pages had been retrieved and some lucky person spent all their working days scanning them into computers. Even if a particular file had been destroyed, there were usually so many cross-references in other documents that it could be reconstructed.

Successive governments had tried to ensure that no traces of the StB remained, but even after thirteen and a half thousand people had been dismissed, a recent trawl had found eight hundred had managed to slip back into the police.

Most former StB officers had just been sacked, but a selection had faced criminal charges as a result of evidence linking them to crimes or abuses, and it was this list that Mucha had been carefully scrutinising.

He had an idea that he remembered one name, and checked on the police computer. Sure enough, the man had been arrested and charged with a serious assault leading to death. A little more delving produced the information that the victim had last been seen entering the Red House in 1985, and that the perpetrator was one of two men who had been jailed for twenty years. It was likely that they had been released, but if they could be found then perhaps one or other of them would be a helpful source of information about what had gone on there.

There was no point in having a name if he could not find the man, though, so Mucha fetched himself some coffee and made himself comfortable for a long session in the databases.

Given that Mucha and Slonský were of similar ages, it was instructive to contrast their attitudes to, and competence with, modern technology.

Slonský was generally not permitted to review security videos until someone had verified that a copy had been made, following the regrettable incident with the "record" button following a supermarket robbery. He relied upon Navrátil to work the DVD player in the Situation Control Room and was never quite sure which of the screens in there was going to show the images he wanted. Until Peiperová came to work for him, he had no idea that his telephone incorporated an answering machine, let alone how to retrieve the messages from it.

Mucha, on the other hand, used the access to databases via the computer terminals at the front desk to good effect. In that respect he did not differ from hundreds of other officers in the Czech Police.

Where he stood out was in his knowledge of the tens of thousands of files that had not yet been computerised, their contents and their whereabouts. And here he played mercilessly on the historical tendency of records officers throughout Prague going back to the early days of Communism, for whom one self-evident truth dictated their approach to requests for access.

If you know a file exists, you're probably entitled to see it.

Westerners had introduced this strange notion of Freedom of Information, the idea that everything ought to be accessible to the citizen unless there were compelling reasons to prevent it. No such idealism had taken hold in the Czech Republic, where the prime purpose of archivists was generally to find a reason why you could not have the documents you wanted; but against that, the really sensitive stuff had always been subject to outright denial of existence. 'You can't have that file because it doesn't exist' had been a staple excuse of records staff for sixty years, but if you knew that it did exist that could only be because you were entitled to know of its existence and, ipso facto, you should be allowed to have it.

Thus it was that Mucha emerged from a dusty warehouse clutching a battered folder relating to a prosecution in the mid-nineties which he tucked under his arm inside a new folder already housing a prison release certificate. He strode back to police headquarters and lost no time in skipping up the stairs to place them in the hands of Captain Slonský.

This was where his plan came slightly adrift, because Captain Slonský was not there, and these were not documents that could just be left on a desk, so Mucha retraced his steps and headed for the canteen. If Slonský was not there either, he could ask Dumpy Anna if she had seen him, secure in the knowledge that it was unlikely that Slonský would go much more than ninety minutes between visits.

As it happened, a familiar figure attracted his attention. Slonský was preparing to go out to find Vlk and since he did not know how long that would take, he thought he ought to top up his blood sugar with a pastry or two first.

'I thought I might find you here,' said Mucha.

'Well, I've noticed that wherever I am, it's always "here",' Slonský replied. 'If I go anywhere else, by the time I get there it's become "here" too.'

'Odd, that. It happens to me too.'

'Maybe we should ask someone about it.'

'Or we could return to the real world and you could devote some attention to the file I have cunningly obtained for you.'

'Did you sign it out?' Slonský asked.

'Of course,' Mucha replied.

'Damn. That means I'll have to remember to return it.'

'No, it means I'll have to remind you to return it.'

'So who's the lucky ex-inmate?' Slonský asked.

'A man by the name of Jiří Holub, ex-captain in the StB.'

'And why does Ex-Captain Holub interest me?'

'Because he was sent to prison for twenty years for the manslaughter of someone he was interrogating in the Red House.'

'Is he still inside?'

'No,' Mucha replied, 'released late last year at the two-thirds point of his sentence and transferred to the Probation and Mediation Service's loving care.'

'Conditional release, then.'

'Six years and eight months left to serve if he is a naughty boy again.'

'Spare me the reading of the file,' Slonský said. 'What did he do?'

'Holub and another officer, Mrázek, arrested someone back in 1985 for anti-state activities. I forget the victim's name, but it's in your file. They were convinced that he had a contact in a Western embassy who was passing and receiving information, so they questioned him to find out who it was. At some point they took him to the Red House to continue the interrogation. This had become necessary because a German journalist had been tipped off about the arrest and was hovering outside the police station asking awkward questions.'

'So they covered Mr X with a blanket and chucked him in the back of a car?' Slonský asked.

'That's a fair summary,' Mucha replied. 'You could almost have been there.'

'Lucky guess. So he arrives at the Red House, and...'

'It seems from the medical evidence that he had an asthma attack brought on by the stress. Holub and Mrázek delayed getting treatment for him, and he died. That's why they were charged with manslaughter, by the way, rather than murder. The beating they'd given him contributed to his distress or shock, but on its own it wouldn't have killed him.'

'It's a deliberate assault that caused him harm from which he died. But for them he'd have been alive the next day. I've have gone for the murder charge myself,' Slonský said.

'That's immaterial. You're not the Prosecutor.'

'No, more's the pity. Things would be very different if I —'

'May I finish?' Mucha interrupted.

'Please do. Just stop waffling and get to the point.'

'They decided the best thing to do was to return the body to the police station and let the police deal with it,' Mucha continued. 'Together they concocted a story that he'd had the attack in the station and died before medical help could arrive. Unfortunately, when the Wall came down and scores were being settled, one of their ex-colleagues decided to deflect attention from his own misdemeanours by shopping them. The denunciation on its own might not have been sufficient, had it not been for the happy chance that someone who knew the victim was on duty at the guard post by the main gate and vividly remembered him being brought in alive twelve hours after he had allegedly died in custody in the police station.'

'That's very clever of him.'

'Their defence lawyer decided to take the line that they had been acting under orders and that the treatment he had received was no different than anyone else, all of whom had survived up until then. It didn't wash with the court and they went down. Mrázek died in prison but Holub survived, and on that nice green slip of paper you've got the address that he told the Probation Officer was where he would be living. So if you want to, you can pay him a visit.'

'Thanks,' said Slonský. 'I'll do that tomorrow.'

'It's only half past four,' Mucha remarked. 'It's not knocking off time yet.'

'I know what time it is. I'm about to go to a pre-arranged interview with General Rezek's son, Petr Vlk.'

'Petr Vlk? The one who used to do the television stuff?'

'The same. Do you want his autograph?'

'No, but if the opportunity arises to give him a kick behind the knee for being a smarmy git, give him another one from me.'

'Have you met him?'

'No, I just took a dislike to him when I first saw him on screen. I don't need to know someone to despise them.'

'I feel the same way sometimes,' Slonský agreed. 'It must be a gift.'

Valentin had already made some enquiries before Slonský met him.

'This way,' he said.

'Hang on,' Slonský responded. 'This is taking us out of the bar.'

'Yes, we're leaving.'

'Allow me to point out that I haven't had a drink. It goes against the grain to leave without having something.'

'We're leaving because Vlk isn't here. According to my sources, he's likely to be in a club in the Old Town.'

'You leave if you want to. I need to lubricate myself for the journey.'

'Well, if you're having one, I'll keep you company. But our quarry may get away.'

'It's just the one. And I got the impression that Vlk likes to settle in for the night.'

'That's true.'

They each took a mouthful of beer and let it roll over their tongues.

'Slightly on the warm side, but not bad,' Slonský judged.

Ten minutes later honour was satisfied and the two men headed for the address that Valentin had gleaned by telephoning Vlk's office and asking where to find him, although the person answering had conceded that Vlk's movements were not always in line with previous notification, especially if someone else was buying the drinks.

The club indicated was not as unsavoury as its address had suggested, boasting an ordinary glass front door rather than a steel shutter, and sufficient light within to be able to see the person opposite without squinting. There were a number of semi-circular bench seats, many of which were filled with groups of young men and women. A glance at the prices led Slonský to suppose that these were upwardly mobile types with limited financial commitments.

Vlk was sitting in one of the curved booths with no company except a squat tumbler containing an amber liquid. Slonský could just about recognise him as the same person he may have seen on television fifteen or so years ago, largely because Vlk's dress sense had not changed in the meantime. He wore a sports jacket and a black roll-neck sweater, slightly flared black trousers and a pair of elastic-sided boots of the kind that had been very popular around the time Slonský got married. Vlk's hair, once jet black but now flecked with grey, was a little too long to be fashionable or, indeed, controllable, so a cantilevered section that had begun the evening lacquered into place had begun to flop downwards as the heat in the club made him sweat.

Despite his substantial consumption, Slonský had not had a drink problem for over thirty years. He would, if pressed, admit that he could not remember much of the years 1971 to 1973 after his wife Věra left him, but aside from that extended period of oblivion, he had been careful to keep within his limits. In this regard he was now assisted by his bladder, which saw to it that he had plenty of exercise walking back and forth to the toilet, but also by a determination never to be out of control. However, he knew the signs of alcohol dependency, and when he looked at Petr Vlk he could see a full set. Although he could only have been drinking for an hour or two, Vlk was looking a little tired and his speech was not as clear as he might have hoped.

Slonský and Valentin introduced themselves and asked if they might join him.

'Ah, company! How delightful,' Vlk replied. 'Please do. It's always pleasant to make new friends.' He raised his glass in salute, drained it, and looked around as if bewildered to find it empty. He lifted a thumb in the direction of the barman. 'How may I help you?' Vlk asked.

'I'm afraid we have some rather sad news for you,' Slonský replied. 'I have to tell you that your sister Adalheid has been killed.'

Vlk blinked as if having some difficulty processing this information. 'Killed? Adalheid?'

'I'm afraid so.'

'Poor girl,' said Vlk. He attempted a brave smile. 'I was rather hoping you were going to tell me the old man had keeled over.'

'I understand you and your father don't see eye to eye,' Slonský said.

'No, that's a fair summary. In fact, it's a bit of an understatement. I can't remember the last time we exchanged a civil word.'

'You and Adalheid had different mothers, I believe?'

'Yes. My father divorced my mother shortly after I was born. She wasn't the right sort of wife for a rising StB officer, you see. Too independent and insufficiently docile. Adalheid's mother was a genuine proletarian, grateful for anything she got. I don't have anything against her — from what I could tell she was a nice woman and devoted to Adalheid — but I could cheerfully see Daddy rot in Hell. The divorce was a calculated business transaction, you see? Where is that fellow with the drinks?'

Valentin went over to the bar where the barman explained that he thought the gentleman might have had enough. On the assurance that Slonský was a police officer who had just brought Vlk news of a death in the family, the barman gave way and a tray of drinks soon arrived, along with Vlk's bill, the traditional Czech way of telling a drinker he was not going to get any more.

'How much?' Vlk exploded. 'For three little Scotches?'

'It says here you've had five,' Slonský explained. 'And they were large ones.'

'They may be large in this bar,' Vlk grumbled, 'but they barely dampened the sides of the glass. You're a police officer. Check his measures, why don't you?'

'Have you eaten?' Slonský suddenly enquired.

'Eaten? I don't think so. No, of course not. It's early yet.'

'Why don't we drink these and go and have an informal bite somewhere, perhaps with something to wash it down?' Slonský gave Vlk his most appealing look, to which Vlk responded with a charming smile.

'How very civil! That's the spirit. And I can tell you a bit more about how much of a bastard my father is.'

'That's what I was hoping,' said Slonský.

Navrátil and Peiperová were strolling back to the barracks where Peiperová lived, having been to the movies to see a film of her choosing. Navrátil's taste ran more to the kind of film that had witty dialogue, and he was very willing to sample any movie made in black and white on the assumption that it must be either old or artistic, whereas Peiperová, for all her practical and modern approach to life, was a devotee of the chick flick.

Along the road in front of them there was a white van which was being loaded by two men with the contents of an apartment. For a moment, Navrátil thought that maybe he should check that they were authorised to do so, just in case he was an unwitting observer of a burglary, but a quick conversation between a woman in the upper window and one of the men put his mind at rest. They closed the back doors of the van, returned to the flat and reappeared a few minutes later with a rolled-up rug which was too long to go inside and had to be secured to the roof. Navrátil suggested to Peiperová that they should cross the road to avoid becoming caught up in the removal process, and they resumed their conversation on the other side.

'He was quite attractive,' Peiperová suggested.

'Good-looking or not, he was unattractive. Neanderthals always are.'

'He just needed taking in hand. If it had worked out, she would have tamed him.'

'Now that's the big difference between the sexes,' Navrátil remarked. 'Women hope the men they marry will change, and men marry women hoping they won't.'

'We're both in for disappointment then,' Peiperová laughed. 'Will you still love me when I'm old and wrinkled?'

Navrátil sensed a trap.

'I love my mother, and she's old and wrinkled,' he answered.

Peiperová laughed, shook her head, and walked on, giving her fiancé a squeeze round his middle and failing to notice the backward glance he gave the van as an idea came to him.

Vlk was relaxed and communicative, a fact probably not wholly unconnected with the empty bottle in the wine cooler. Slonský had carefully sidestepped any questions about Vlk's television work, but Valentin had agreed that it was of the highest order, considering the constraints that Vlk had to work under.

Valentin had no idea what these might have been, but he knew that every television presenter in current affairs believes that they are being held back by petty restrictions and needs little encouragement to share them at length, which Vlk duly did, leading Slonský to feel that whereas he had previously believed that the Czech police had cornered the market in incompetent management, there was actually some in the broadcasting world too, suggesting that the seam of incompetence that could be mined was much larger than he had thought.

He allowed Vlk to rant right through the main course and coffee — nobody wanted a dessert — before asking him the pertinent questions that were the purpose of the outing.

'Do you know exactly what your father did in the StB?'

'He was a political officer here in Prague,' Vlk replied. 'It was his job to clamp down on dissidents.'

'When did he retire?'

'He would argue that he never got the chance, because he was one of the officers kicked out in 1990 when the StB was dissolved. He was prepared to sign the pledge of allegiance to the new regime, unlike some of his colleagues, but they didn't offer him any alternative job. Damn good thing too. He should have been one of those who were prosecuted.'

'Why?'

'I don't know anything particular, just his general attitude to people who were arguing for reform. I'm going to sound like an awful hypocrite, because I can't deny that my father's influence must have opened some doors for me. I didn't ask for that, but people chose to be co-operative rather than get on the wrong side of an StB general.'

'I wonder why?' Slonský mused, earning a smirk from Vlk.

'He could be incredibly vindictive. Of course, that's what made him good at his job, though it didn't do much for his parenting skills.'

'I understand the two of you fell out in a big way,' Valentin continued.

'That's one way of putting it. Around 1992, my employers produced a series of documentaries about the work of the StB under Communism. Dad was mauled in one of them, and he thought I should have tipped him off and had them suppressed. He was a dinosaur and didn't seem to understand that the days when you could ring a producer and just order him to burn a film had long gone. After all, if Dad couldn't do it, why should he think I could?'

'And you fell out over that?' Slonský persisted, with just a hint of "I wasn't born yesterday" in his tone.

'Things got a bit heated and I said that if that was what he'd done then the public ought to hear about it and he ought to be in jail. I'd rather draw a veil over the rest of that particular conversation, if you don't mind, except to say that it ended with us in complete agreement. Each of us thought the other ought to be ashamed of himself.'

'What did your sister think?' Slonský asked.

'Adalheid was always a daddy's girl when she was growing up, but it wasn't actually about his power or status with her, just a daddy-daughter thing like plenty of other families. Like a mediaeval king with a princess to marry off, Dad was on the lookout for a suitable catch for her. It wouldn't work with me, because any woman was bound to have less influence than a man, but if he could marry her to the son of someone important in the Party it would give his career a boost.'

'Did you ever marry?' Slonský continued.

Vlk looked at them sadly. 'No, I chose not to play that game.'

'What game is that?'

'The sad old queen marrying a bit of fluff to cover up his interest in young men game. I wasn't made for married life. That was another thing Dad held against me. He reckoned I'd been spoiled by my mother — who was pretty much a saint, by the way, struggling to bring me up with the occasional handout from him. He had visitation rights as part of the divorce settlement but hardly ever exercised them. I might see him a dozen times a year, I suppose.'

'But he helped you with your career?'

'Yes, he put in a few calls to get me a start. He said it would reflect badly on the family — by which he meant himself — if I loafed around doing nothing. But he made plain that all I was getting was a foot in the door. Anything beyond that I'd have to earn for myself. And I did.'

Since it all came tumbling down when your father was sacked, that's a matter for debate, thought Slonský, but he decided not to antagonise Vlk. 'Adalheid married quite young, I think,' he said.

'The son of a Deputy Minister of the Interior. Absolute sponge. My God, people say *I* drink, but at least I stay upright and I take a taxi home. He didn't, hence his sticky end. He got tanked up and drove his BMW into the supporting column of a bridge at around ninety kilometres an hour. Since it was a built-up area it was damn lucky he did, or he'd have killed some other poor soul. But she'd given up on him before that. His family claimed he turned to drink after she rejected him, so it was all her fault, but that nicely overlooks the fact that he was so hammered on his wedding day that he thought he'd married one of the bridesmaids and tried to get her to go upstairs with him before spending the night sleeping on the landing. She divorced him.'

'With your father's blessing?' Slonský asked.

'He saw it as inevitable by then. He'd sent her back a couple of times when she'd turned up at home with a shiner after her husband hit her, but when she said she'd rather kill herself than live with him, Dad gave way. She paid for it, though. Until the Wall came down her father-in-law saw to it that she didn't get a decent job.' Vlk looked longingly at the empty wine bottle, causing Slonský to suggest a small schnapps for the road. 'What a splendid fellow you are,' opined Vlk, 'looking after a chap after such a sad event. Here's to Adalheid!'

He raised his glass, to which Slonský and Valentin responded by repeating the toast.

'If only we could all get along like we are tonight,' Vlk murmured.

Slonský could see that Vlk was beginning to slip off the Peak of Volubility and was heading for either the Trough of Insensibility or the Weepy Place of Sentimentality, so he pressed for a few more snippets of information.

'Had you seen Adalheid recently?'

'She came round for my birthday in January, bless her. She brought me a very acceptable bottle of rioja and a sweater. She was a good sort, you know. After Mother died she was the only one of them who bothered with me. Dad didn't even come to the funeral, but she did. Who could have wanted to harm such an angel?' His eyes glazed and he sniffled loudly. 'Whoever he is, he's a bastard,' he declared.

Chapter 7

Navrátil arrived for work at ten to seven the following morning, but even with such an early arrival he could only take third place in the office race, because Krob and Slonský were already at their desks. A few minutes later Jerneková appeared for the morning briefing which, for largely historic reasons, always took place in the men's office, followed by Peiperová, who had correctly anticipated a general desire for coffee and was carrying a tray. In her days as an ordinary officer, Peiperová had resented repeatedly being sent to fetch coffee, but now that she had been promoted to Lieutenant and did not need to do it, she was very happy to volunteer.

As a Captain, Slonský could have asked the canteen staff to deliver coffee to his office but as he told Dumpy Anna, such an abuse of his rank would be unforgivable and would deprive him of the pleasure of seeing her happy smiling face every day. 'Get away with you!' she had replied, before slipping him the last of the roast pork in a roll. The two of them enjoyed a prolonged friendship that was entirely confined to working hours. Dumpy Anna liked a man who enjoyed her food, and Slonský, who believed that the canteen was the beating heart of an efficient police force (because who can detect on an empty stomach?) regarded her as the heart's pacemaker without which nothing would happen.

'Did you have a successful evening, sir?' Navrátil enquired.

'That depends on whether Colonel Rajka approves my expenses, lad. Vlk has expensive tastes. But I think we did. Jerneková, Adalheid was once married. Find out what you can about her husband. He died in a car crash around 1986. See if we've got any information about it on file.'

'You think there's something suspicious about it, sir?' Jerneková asked.

'No, but we'd look a bit stupid if there was and we hadn't even asked the question, wouldn't we? It's just that the StB were really good at rigging bogus car crashes. They didn't always remember to remove the handcuffs securing the deceased to the steering wheel, but that's a small detail.'

Jerneková scribbled a note in her pad.

'Sir,' Navrátil said, 'I've got an idea and I wanted to see if you thought it was sensible.'

'Yours usually are, Navrátil.'

'It's just that when Lieutenant Peiperová and I were walking back from the cinema last night, we saw a family moving house and it spurred a line of thought about how the murderer got the body over the wall.'

'Why — did they have a trampoline?'

'No, sir, they had an oversized rug.'

'I'm listening, lad,' Slonský announced, managing to convey that he was sceptical about the value of the notion Navrátil was about to expound.

'The rug wouldn't fit in the van, sir.'

'Big rug, small van, I assume.'

'That's right.'

'Then they needed a bigger van. Well, that's that conundrum solved.'

'That's not the point I wanted to make, sir.'

'No?'

'No. They transported the rug by attaching it to the roof. Now, we know Adalheid Rezeková was wrapped in a carpet or rug at some point. Suppose the killer wrapped her in a rug and put her on the roof of a vehicle. Then, when he gets to the Red House he drives up the side lane, parks as close to the wall as he can, and swings the carpet round so one end is on top of the wall. Then all he has to do is push and she'll drop over the other side.'

Slonský had a good scratch of his ear while he pictured the scene in his head. 'Not a bad idea, Navrátil. But there's one difficulty. You've accounted for how he could get a body off a vehicle, but how would he get it on top of the vehicle in the first place? It's as difficult to lift it onto a van as it is to put it on the wall.'

'Not if he lives in an upstairs flat,' Peiperová chipped in.

'Right,' Slonský said, 'Navrátil and Krob, I want you to get yourself down to the Red House and look out for any video cameras that might have caught an image of someone driving around with a carpet on their roof at night. Spread out over a wide area, at least up to the nearest major road junction in each direction. Secure the videos for the nights of that weekend if you can. Then when you get back, you can enjoy watching them all till you prove Navrátil right.'

'What do you want me to do, sir?' Peiperová enquired.

'I want you to talk to anyone you can find who knew Adalheid. See if anyone knows if she was seeing someone, but first I think you need to turn her flat over. There may be some clues there. Jerneková, when you've finished your first job, give your boss a hand. All clear?'

Everyone assented.

'Meanwhile, I'm going to see how an ex-offender is getting settled back into the world.'

Slonský completely understood the suspicion with which he was regarded by Jiří Holub when the latter finally opened the door and discovered the identity of his visitor.

'What do you want?' Holub snapped.

'A nice quiet chat,' Slonský replied, 'here or at a café of your choosing. I want to pick your brains.'

'A public place would be good, in case you turn nasty.'

'Being in a public place won't stop me turning nasty, but take my word for it I won't.'

Holub considered for a moment, then lifted his jacket off a hook and closed the door behind him. 'There's a place down the street where we can talk.'

'Lead on, then.'

Holub showed no curiosity in the purpose of Slonský's visit until they were both sitting with a coffee and a ham roll. Even then, Slonský saw no reason to put off a ham roll to give an explanation, so it was not until both rolls had vanished that he opened up about his interest.

'This is not about anything you may or may not have done,' he began. 'I'm interested, as one old-timer to another, about how the StB worked back in those days. I can't tell you exactly why just yet, but it's to do with a present-day case.'

Holub nodded. 'The judge said I should have disobeyed my orders. Well, he can say that sitting on a bench a decade later. You and I know what happened to officers who didn't obey orders. They finished up checking passports or guarding a work camp — and that's if they were lucky. I had a wife and two kids to look after.' He took a noisy slurp of coffee. 'The boys don't speak to me now. My wife waited, but I can't get a job to keep her properly either. I've paid for my loyalty to the StB.'

'I know,' Slonský said gently. 'But I'd draw a distinction between people who were just trying to do their job and those who enjoyed beating people up, wouldn't you?'

Holub eyed Slonský suspiciously as if trying to determine whether this was a veiled challenge before deciding it was a valid argument. 'I knew plenty of those. I wasn't one of them, though.'

'I didn't say you were. Was Mrázek handy with his fists?'

'He wasn't the worst, but he liked to give people a couple of taps to check they were taking him seriously. The bloke who died wasn't actually treated that badly. He wasn't given food or drink and we threatened him a bit, maybe slapped him a few times, but we didn't use a baton on him or anything like that. That's why we took him to the Red House, where we could have been more physical.'

'Tell me more about the Red House. We've found a body in its grounds, and I'm curious to know why the murderer dumped her there. It's as if it meant something to him, because he took quite a chance taking her there.'

'You think he may have been beaten up there?'

'It crossed my mind. I know it's been nearly twenty years since the place was last used, but someone who was twenty or thirty then could be the man we're looking for.'

Holub signalled the waiter to refill his cup, so Slonský did likewise.

'The Red House had two busy periods,' explained Holub. 'It was used a lot before the Prague Spring, especially in the fifties, then it went quiet during the reforms. It was only really in the seventies when the regime thought they were secure enough to start stamping out dissidents that it came back into fashion. Between, say, 1970 and 1975 the place saw a lot of activity, or so I heard. But after that we only took the occasional person there.'

'What does "occasional" mean? One a week? One a month?'

'There might be three or four inmates at a time. We'd soften them up, then when we'd finished with them we'd hand them back to the ordinary police.'

'What about the ones who died?'

'What do you mean, the ones who died?'

'Exactly that. We know there were bodies buried in the grounds of the Red House. Do you know who they could be?'

Holub shook his head vigorously. 'I never knew that to happen. I mean, people died, but generally they were sent for cremation straight away. The one who died in front of us we just returned to the police station because there was hardly a mark on him.'

Slonský decided to take Holub into his confidence. 'The odd thing about the case I'm working on is that the dead woman was laid to rest on top of someone else's grave. I'm assuming there won't be records anywhere telling me who was underneath, so my best bet is finding someone who remembers the incident.'

'If I could help, I would,' Holub replied. 'It wouldn't do me any harm in the eyes of the Probation Officer. But I can honestly say I never knew anyone buried in the grounds.'

'Do you have any idea why it might have happened?'

Holub sipped his coffee as he reflected. 'It would be someone they didn't want to admit having had in the first place. Someone who would have had people looking for him.'

'But then there'd be a fuss if he didn't reappear, surely?'

'Not necessarily. Towards the end of the Communist years, people were bolder, but in the seventies sometimes dissidents slipped over the border and didn't want anyone to know where they were in case it put their remaining families at risk. They'd go ahead to find a safe place then send for their wives and children.'

'Okay, I can remember that happening occasionally.'

'But sometimes a while would elapse before they could get a message to the family, who would naturally not be drawing attention to the fact that their man had gone in case he hadn't yet crossed the border. So it could be some weeks or months before they realised something must have gone wrong. And all that mattered to the StB was that nothing could be pinned on them, so if they just said they knew nothing about it, who could prove them wrong?'

'That means they must have managed to arrest someone without it coming to anyone's attention.'

'That's not impossible. We didn't always kick doors in at two in the morning, you know.'

Slonský smiled ruefully. 'It seemed to me that I did. You didn't get a lot of sleep as a junior officer back then.'

'People think we did it all the time, but the main reason for doing it was that they would be at home. If we could find them earlier in the day we'd arrest them then, especially if we could take them by surprise. We'd quite often arrest artistic types as they left the theatre or ballet, because they weren't expecting it and they might well have had a few drinks. I nicked a footballer in the dressing room after he'd been substituted because he was there on his own.'

Slonský debated whether he could take Holub into his confidence a little further, but was taken by surprise when Holub suddenly asked a direct question.

'Anyway, you keep saying the body was a woman. No woman ever worked in the Red House, and I don't remember more than one or two being taken there, so what connection could there be?'

'She's the daughter of a former high-ranking StB officer.'

Holub called for another coffee and stirred it slowly as he thought. 'So you think she was killed in revenge for something he did?'

'Not necessarily, but until I find a better motive for someone to kill her that seems the favourite to me. Obviously the Red House is important to the killer. It seems likely that her father worked in the Red House. So in the absence of any other clear motive, that's the one I have to run with. I haven't closed my mind to others — but in any crime, you investigate the bit that stands out and makes it different.'

Holub gulped back a mouthful of coffee. 'Are you going to tell me who it is?'

'It'll be in the papers soon enough, I suppose. She's the daughter of General Rezek.'

'Rezek? Is he still alive? I wish you luck. You won't be short of people who wanted him dead. But why not kill him? Why his daughter?'

'I don't know,' Slonský replied. 'And I'm not even sure I'm right in the first place. Nor do I know why he's waited this long to take his revenge, and until I can answer those questions I don't have much of a case. Until I know whose body was in that grave with her, I don't know where to start looking.'

'Can't you get those clever fellows at the medical school to reconstruct the face from the skull?'

'I could, if I had a skull. The first body was taken away, presumably when the second one was left.'

Holub sniffed. 'I wouldn't want to be in your shoes. Things were much simpler in my day. Dead people stayed where they were put.'

'They usually do these days too. This is a new one on me.' Slonský fished in his wallet and handed over a couple of banknotes. 'This is for your time. If you remember anything that might give me a steer on that body, I'd be grateful for a call.'

Holub accepted the notes and tucked them carefully in a pocket. 'I wouldn't normally take money off a policeman, but times aren't easy.'

'I know. Whatever you did, you've paid for it. I'm as happy as anyone else to see offenders put away but once they've served their sentence, they need a chance to start again. And they usually don't get it in this country.'

Holub frowned. 'This grave — where was it?'

'Near the south wall, where the hothouse used to be.'

'I might be able to give you a bit of help. I think there may have been something under the ground there when I first went there in 1973. We had some dogs, and I remember they used to kick up when they were taken to that area. I once asked what was spooking them, and my sergeant said some questions are better not asked.'

'Is he still around?'

'No idea. Name of Jelínek. If he's still alive he must be into his eighties or even older.'

'First name?'

Holub smiled for the first time. 'In my day you didn't address sergeants by their first name. I've no idea.'

Navrátil and Krob were not having much luck. There were very few security cameras on the roads leading to the Red House, and those that existed were uninformative. It was boring work, because forty-eight hours of video footage from each camera takes around forty-eight hours to watch, and even if it was run at a faster speed there was a limit imposed by the ability of the eye to take it all in.

It was not until tape eleven that Krob found something. A van came into view with a carpet on the roof. The driver could not be seen clearly, partly because he was driving around shortly before midnight with sunglasses on, but Krob was able to get a registration number for the vehicle.

Krob called for Navrátil to check his findings and was instructed to look at the vehicle licensing database to get the name and address of the owner. Krob did so, and came back to Navrátil's desk looking perplexed.

'It belongs to Prague City Council,' he said. 'It's one of those electric street-cleaning cars.'

'I didn't think they could go that quick,' Navrátil replied.

'They can't, when they're cleaning. They're restricted to about twelve kilometres per hour. But when the brushes are retracted, they can manage normal car speeds.'

'Call TSK and see where that vehicle is now. There may be some forensic material on it, so we need to get it out of service.'

Krob rang TSK, which was the company tasked with cleaning Prague's streets. Technically, it was not the City Council, but a company wholly owned by the City Council, though Krob was not clear what real difference that might make. Within ten minutes they rang back to say that they had tracked that vehicle down and it was returning to base in Prague's Ninth District. Krob copied down the address and he and Navrátil drove out to look it over.

Krob had taken a copy of the screen shot showing the van with the carpet on top.

'I don't understand,' said the depot manager. 'Why would one of our vehicles be out at that time of night?'

'We assume it had been borrowed,' Navrátil explained. 'But wasn't it missed?'

The manager leafed through the work log. 'There you are,' he said, pointing to an entry. 'Unit 46 was discovered to be flat in the morning, but this was explained because the charging point had not been turned on.'

'Wouldn't that be unusual?' Navrátil persisted.

'Almost unknown. It's a routine action. At the end of the day the vehicles are parked by their chargers and the staff walk along plugging them in and turning them on. I've never known one to miss one before. But why not just plug it in and charge it again?'

Krob had an idea about that. 'Maybe there wasn't time to fully charge it, which would have caused some questions to be asked. It would be much easier to give the impression that it had never been charged in the first place.'

Navrátil was more concerned about a different point. 'Aren't your vehicles locked away at night?' he asked.

'Who would want to steal a street-cleaning machine? They're not exactly the go-to vehicle for joyriders. They're behind a barrier arm, but I suppose you could just drive up onto the grass and leave by driving round the barrier.'

'You might want to reconsider your security arrangements,' Navrátil suggested. 'Meanwhile, we'll have to take Unit 46 out of service while our forensic technicians examine it.'

The depot manager winced. 'We hosed them all down on Friday evening,' he said. 'But of course you're welcome to do whatever you need.'

For once Slonský did not ask Mucha to track down Jelínek. This was partly due to his secretive nature, but mainly to the fact that Mucha was having a few days' leave. Slonský was not a great lover of leave, because there was nowhere he would rather be than at work, unless he could find someone prepared to pay him to sit in bars, but he accepted that even Mucha was entitled to a few days now and again. If only he had a telephone number for Mucha's wife's sister, because he could be sure that if the Evil Witch of Kutná Hora dropped in for a visit Mucha would find an urgent reason why he needed to go to work again.

Slonský knocked politely on the door of the Human Resources Department. For once he was visiting during office hours, in defiance of his usual practice, which was to turn up when everyone had gone home. This was possible because the Duty Sergeants had a key in their safe that allowed access to these sensitive records in case of fire. One lunchtime Slonský took that key for a little walk to a nearby locksmith, and it returned with a twin brother which was currently taped to the underside of Krob's desk. To Slonský's way of thinking, the problem with requesting information from HR through official channels was that until he had a squint at the files he had no idea whether they had information that would justify all the form-filling that he would have to do. It was much more efficient to take a peek himself, then when he knew exactly what he wanted he could ask for it and save the HR staff some time by only requesting those particular files.

In this case, he explained to the clerk who admitted him that he was looking for contact details for a former staff member called Jelínek.

'When did he retire?' the clerk asked.

'I don't know exactly, but around twenty years ago. He was still working in 1973 if that helps.'

'It doesn't really. Do you know his rank?'

'Sergeant. In 1973, that is.'

'And the Directorate in which he worked?'

'StB.'

The clerk stiffened. 'We don't actually have the StB records here.'

'No, but when a company is sold to another company the staff go with it, right?'

'Yes...'

'So presumably the staff records go with the staff?'

'Yes, normally...'

'So if the StB is absorbed into the ordinary police, the police would need access to StB records?'

'Yes. I can see where this is leading,' the clerk replied. 'We don't have the records themselves, but we do have access to the catalogue that tells us whether we have any records, though I can't promise we can share them.'

'Splendid. That would be a great start,' Slonský exclaimed enthusiastically.

'I'll have to use the terminal in the back office,' the clerk said. 'Access is restricted for obvious reasons.'

'Of course,' said Slonský, who had been musing to himself whether a nocturnal visit would serve any purpose given that the chances were that the files were protected with a password, and it was unlikely to be 1234 as on his own little-used terminal.

The clerk took his notepad and left Slonský alone. Alone, that is, except for the computer terminal that he had been using and on which he remained logged in. It was the work of a moment for Slonský to see if he could improve his computing knowledge by successfully calling up his own personnel record. To his surprise, it was quite easy. All he needed to do was to type his surname in the box marked "Surname", because there were no other Slonskýs past or present in the police files, and in no time he was browsing his own profile.

He had previously done some judicious editing of the disciplinary section of his paper file, so there was no advantage in changing any of that, but the idea came to him that he might be able to ease the strain that he was feeling as a result of approaching the retirement age of 63 by making a small change to the record. Where his date of birth ended in 1947, he carefully moved the cursor across and altered it to 1949. When he had done so, a helpful little box jumped up to warn him to save his change before leaving; not only that, it was kind enough to let him know that he could do so by hitting the F10 key. Slonský tried hitting the F, the 1 and the 0, but that did not seem to work; but in a triumph of customer service, the program had anticipated this possibility and another little box showed him where the F10 key was. By the time the clerk returned, Slonský was two years younger and the terminal had been returned to the main menu.

'I think this may be your man,' the clerk announced, pushing an index card towards Slonský.

'Jelínek, Bohumil, born 28 March 1922, Senior Sergeant, StB, until 1985. Sounds like a good start. Is he still alive?'

'I hope so, because we're paying him a pension,' the clerk simpered.

'Then this must be his current address,' Slonský decided, and copied it into his notebook. He bounded down the stairs feeling very pleased with himself and decided to celebrate his two lost birthdays with a cream cake somewhere.

Chapter 8

Jerneková was scathing about Adalheid Rezeková's underwear drawer. 'These cannot be comfortable,' she remarked. 'The things women wear to please men.'

'So far as we know, she didn't have a man,' said Peiperová, 'so we have to conclude she wore these for herself.'

'In my books, underwear is there to hold everything in and keep it where you put it,' Jerneková replied. She held up a lavender lace thong. 'This is more like trying to carry jelly in a string bag.'

'We're not here to appraise her fashion choices,' Peiperová snapped. 'Keep your eyes open for anything that may help with our enquiries. In particular, let's look for a diary and any letters.'

Peiperová had been well trained. However sloppy or casual Slonský might appear to be, he was a meticulous and diligent searcher, and he had passed these characteristics on to his juniors. They approached searching rather differently, Navrátil preferring to conduct a quick skim of the premises first and then concentrate his efforts once he knew what he was dealing with, whereas Peiperová worked more slowly but concluded each room before starting the next. It was the first time Jerneková had been detailed to conduct a search, and Peiperová was concerned that she might overlook something in her haste to find useful material.

'Don't forget to look for anything that isn't in a drawer,' Peiperová counselled. 'Things at the back of drawers, tucked under a blotter or between books. Take your time.'

It was Peiperová who found a diary in a large shoulder bag, presumably the one Rezeková used for work, but there were no private appointments in it. However, there was a tantalising hint that an appointment had existed, because she had blocked out the first half of the Thursday morning before she was found. Did this mean that she had been expecting to be staying out late the night before?

Jerneková had turned her attention to the mail and the refrigerator. It looked as if the unopened post would probably have been delivered on or after Friday.

'The absence of post delivered on Thursday isn't conclusive,' Peiperová remarked. 'There may simply have been none.'

'Her milk went out of date on Sunday. There isn't a lot in the fridge, to be honest. Maybe she wasn't a keen cook.'

'Perhaps she would have done her food shopping at the weekend. The dirty plate looks to me like a breakfast plate. It's not big enough for it to be an evening meal.'

'So it may be that she had a dinner date on Wednesday evening and never came home?'

'It looks that way. But don't forget we don't have any hard evidence. We're arguing from things we're not finding — a gap in the diary, no evidence of an evening meal, post that wasn't opened. After all, do you always open mail on the day it arrives?'

'Yes, actually I do. I don't get much post, and what I get is often from debt collection agencies. You don't want to ignore those bastards,' Jerneková replied.

Slonský was in a good mood as he entered the office, which was swiftly dissipated by the message Krob had for him.

'Colonel Rajka says he'd like to see you when you get back.'

'Did he say why?'

'No, sir. He didn't sound very happy, though.'

'Right-ho. I'll just get a coffee and then go and see him.'

Krob coughed in embarrassment. 'The Colonel said I was to stop you going for a coffee first, sir. In fact, he said I wasn't to let you go anywhere where you could spend money.'

Thus chastened, Slonský walked downstairs and into the lush carpeting of the executive wing which housed his boss, Colonel Rajka. Rajka had previously been head of the Office of Internal Inspection, the body that looked into the conduct of police officers, and when he had been promoted to replace Colonel Urban, Rajka had tried to persuade Slonský to take over at OII. Slonský could not deny that there were attractions. He loathed police corruption and those who practised it, and had already been largely responsible for putting a number of police officers behind bars. It would have come with a bigger salary and a promotion to Major. On the other hand, the officers in OII were unable to socialise with colleagues. They were required to keep a proper distance between themselves and those they might be called upon to investigate. And, with the possible exception of Rajka himself, they were astoundingly dull and humourless.

As for Rajka, it was a very unusual experience for Slonský to have a senior officer over him whom he both liked and respected. They could never be close friends, of course, so long as Rajka maintained the aversion to alcohol and caffeine that he had nurtured since his days as an Olympic wrestler. He looked well on it, and if Slonský ever wanted a telephone directory torn in half he knew exactly where he would go, but the idea of sitting down with a mate to share a brew of green tea filled Slonský with horror. To him, not drinking beer was unpatriotic. Admittedly he had seen the famous clip of Rajka standing on the rostrum in tears as the Czech flag was raised, so he had to concede that it was possible to love the Czech Republic without raising a half-litre tankard to it, but he told himself that Rajka would have been a beer-drinker if his training regimen had allowed it, so that was all right.

Rajka glanced up as Slonský knocked at the open door. 'Come in, so long as there's no charge.'

'This is about my expenses claim, isn't it, sir?'

'They don't call you Prague's number one detective for nothing, do they, Slonský?'

'I don't think they do call me that, sir. Surely that's you?'

'Cut the flattery. Just how many people did you take to dinner?'

'There were just the three of us, sir. Me, Petr Vlk and Valentin.'

'Valentin? What was he doing there?'

'It was a sort of finder's fee for tracking down Vlk.'

'Vlk and Valentin. Two journalists. Well, I suppose that explains the drinks bill.'

'It was just to get Vlk talking, sir. I needed to know about his father.'

'Yes, I've read your report. Isn't it a bit early in the game to be concluding that it's a revenge killing for something her father did?'

'I haven't definitely concluded that, sir. It's just the first option given that we don't know of anyone else who might have had a motive to kill her.'

Rajka sat back and thought for a moment. 'And did Vlk come up trumps?'

'Not really. He confirmed what we already knew, fleshed out the family background, but there was little new material that was directly relevant.'

Rajka signed off the expenses sheet. 'Okay, you win some, you lose some. Just don't make a habit of spending that much on one witness, please.'

'I won't, sir.'

'You recall when I got this job I offered you my old one?'

'Yes, sir. I turned it down, if I remember correctly.'

'You do. You haven't reconsidered?'

'No, sir. I'm a criminal detective. It's what I do, and I'm a bit old to learn new tricks.'

'When you leave here, you might want to drop in on my old office and say hello to my replacement.'

This was news to Slonský; and, as he ascertained via a brisk detour to the front desk, it was news to Mucha too.

'I can't believe it,' said Mucha. 'They've appointed a new head of OII and neither of us knew?'

'Are we losing our grip?' Slonský pondered. 'Or are the top brass getting cleverer?'

Mucha shot him an old-fashioned look. 'The top brass getting cleverer? How likely is that?'

'Yes, you're right. I mean, I hadn't even heard any rumours.'

'That's because I hadn't got round to starting any.'

'Well, I suppose I'd better go on my fact-finding mission. I'll report back later.'

To find Rajka's old office, it was necessary to walk to the end of the senior officers' corridor and then descend a small flight of stairs into the end of the wing. There was a security door where you were identified, this being a device to ensure that the senior officers could not put pressure on the Office of Internal Inspection team. For convenience, the security door was often propped open but it was guarded by a woman secretary who acted as the equivalent of a rottweiler but with fewer social graces.

Slonský was allowed to pass and entered the office where he received the biggest surprise he had known for some time. Behind the desk sat the spitting image of his old boss, Captain Lukas. Slonský would have been completely taken in by this impostor were it not for the error that saw him decked out in a major's uniform.

'Slonský! How very kind of you to drop in on my very first day,' said Lukas.

'Is that really you, sir?'

'You look like you've seen a ghost. Yes, it's me. Colonel Rajka was kind enough to suggest that I might come back for a short while when he was promoted and you refused the job.'

'But I thought you were enjoying retirement?'

Lukas looked slightly awkward. 'My wife and daughters are delightful, but I missed male company. And when Rajka said that he felt that Captain Bendík was well able to conduct the enquiries but would benefit from the oversight of an experienced officer, I don't mind admitting that I found the suggestion very enticing. So I agreed to come back part-time for six months in the first instance. I'm only going to be here for a couple of days a week, but Bendík and his colleagues can ring me any time if they want me.'

'I'm sure they'll benefit from your support as much as I always did, sir.'

'That's very generous of you,' said Lukas, completely failing to notice that the sentiment was ambiguous. 'And of course the offer of a promotion to major means that when I draw my pension, it will be enhanced. I must admit that I never thought I would ever wear a major's uniform.'

You and me both, thought Slonský.

Bohumil Jelínek may have been eighty-five, but he was just as suspicious as a man half his age.

'Why this sudden interest in my time in the StB?' he asked Slonský. 'Haven't you jailed your quota of ex-officers?'

'I'm not interested in what you did or didn't do. I'm interested in what you know,' Slonský explained.

'I don't think I know anything you'd want to know.'

'Why don't you let me ask, and then you can tell me, and perhaps I'll go away. Unless I think you're lying, in which case I'll move into your spare bedroom and stay until I get the truth.'

'Good luck with that. I haven't got a spare bedroom,' said Jelínek. 'You can have the dog's kennel if you like.'

'I've had worse.'

Jelínek shrugged. 'You'd best come in, then. Mind the dog crap.'

'When you offered me the kennel, I thought the dog must have passed on.'

'It has, but the cleaner's an idle cow.' He shuffled along the hallway and pushed a door open. 'In there. Sit wherever you want.'

Since there was only one armchair, which showed every sign of being Jelínek's preferred seat, Slonský sat on one of the chairs by the dining table.

'I'm here about the Red House,' he began. 'A body has been found there, and one possible line of enquiry is that the victim was killed in revenge for something that her father, an StB officer, may have done in the past.'

'Who was he?' barked Jelínek.

'A man called Rezek.'

'I knew him. Not one of the worst, but not someone you'd get on the wrong side of. He was like a hunting dog. Once he got his teeth into you, he wouldn't let go.'

'Is it possible that someone he arrested died there?'

'It's certainly possible. He wasn't a gentle interrogator. But if you're going to ask me who it was, I can't help you. I don't know any names.'

'Someone we spoke to said he remembered that dogs didn't like to go near the south wall and that, when he mentioned it to you, you told him to keep his nose out.'

'That was generally good advice to anyone where StB business was concerned. It doesn't mean that I knew anything.'

'But you know something about that particular burial, don't you?'

Jelínek dipped his head onto his chest while he had a good think. After a while Slonský began to worry that he may have fallen asleep, but he stirred and began to speak again. 'I said I don't know anything specific, and I stand by that. But during 1970, there was something going on. These were people who were followers of Dubček and his clique, reformers, counter-revolutionaries, you know the sort. Three men were brought to the Red House one night. I don't know who they were and I made it my business not to find out. There was talk that they had been in contact with West Germany and were lobbying the West Germans to stop cosying up to the East Germans. The German Democratic Republic increasingly relied on the money and trade the West Germans were prepared to give them, so the threat was taken very seriously, though I don't know if the three had any real chance of pulling off their plan.

'Anyway, the powers that be wanted to know who they had been talking to and what promises had been made, and Rezek was given the job of finding out. I suppose they were there nine or ten days, then they were gone. But there was a digger on site at the time that had been uprooting the footings of the old glasshouse, and we noticed that it had been used to carve a trench near the south wall.'

'How big a trench?'

'Not very wide — it was only a small digger — but around twenty metres long. We all pretended not to notice it and just got on with our work, but the dogs barked like hell when they went past it.'

'And you've no idea who the three men were?'

'None at all. I assume all three died or were killed, because if any of them had survived he'd have kicked up a racket once the old regime was gone.'

Slonský didn't like the sound of this. Could there really be two more bodies under those flower beds?

Slonský returned to the office under a cloud to find Navrátil in a feverish state.

'There's been a development,' Navrátil announced excitedly.

'Have you been drinking something with artificial food colouring again?' Slonský demanded.

'No. Will you listen while I explain?'

'My lips are sealed. For now.'

'General Rezek came while you were out. He demanded to be taken to the place where his daughter's body was found so that he could leave some flowers there.'

'Did he actually have any flowers?'

'Yes. Roses. Dark red ones.'

'Fine. Proceed.'

'Obviously we had to comply, because it was a reasonable request from a grieving father.'

'Not a very common one, though. I've known it with road accidents, but not usually with murders.'

'But it's not unknown, is it, sir? Anyway, I agreed and I drove him over there. He walked to the spot with me and laid the flowers there, then we bowed our heads for a few moments. He looked around and said that returning to the Red House after so many years brought back some memories, not all of them good ones.'

'I can understand that.'

'Then he thanked me and offered his hand, so I shook it. He marched off, but not the way we'd come. He walked across the lawn to the path.'

'Did he now? And why do you think he did that?'

'I think he wanted to fix exactly where the grave was in relation to the building.'

'And I think you're probably right because I think that too.'

'Sir, I got the impression that he may know whose body was in that grave and that's why he wanted to see exactly where she was.'

Slonský frowned. 'Could we continue this discussion in the canteen? My stomach thinks my throat has been cut.'

They queued to collect a coffee and Slonský put a couple of pastries on a plate.

'If those are both for you, you can put one back,' said Dumpy Anna. 'You told me to stop you overdoing the calories.'

'One of them is for the boy,' Slonský replied.

Dumpy Anna fixed Navrátil with her best basilisk stare. 'The young lieutenant is incapable of telling a lie, so I'm going to ask him to tell me to my face that one of these is for him.'

Slonský sighed and pushed one of the pastries back onto the tray. 'You're a hard woman.'

'I'm only doing what you told me.'

'Why? Nobody else does.'

Slonský and Navrátil found a table and resumed their conversation.

'So you think Rezek knows whose body was buried there before, and therefore he will have some idea who might be behind the killing of his daughter?'

'I don't have any real evidence, sir, but I've just got a feeling.'

'At last. That instinct is the most vital thing in a detective's armoury, lad.'

'I thought you told me diligence was the most vital thing, sir?'

'That's right. They're both the most vital thing. And there are others. But I need to explain what I discovered from the old sergeant I've been to see. He tells me there were three people who disappeared while in custody at the Red House around 1970. He believes that all three were buried in the grounds in a line along that wall.'

'So there are still two to find?'

'If he's right, that seems to be the case. I'll have to apply for an exhumation order to investigate.'

'Are you sure, sir? You'd need an order if you knew there were bodies there, but since we don't know that for sure, and we don't know who they are anyway, so we couldn't put names on the forms, I'd have thought we could do some preliminary digging without an order.'

'I knew there was a reason why I took you on, despite my natural suspicion of people with law degrees.'

'If you've met many of my classmates, I could understand that suspicion, sir.'

'Right! Let's get Novák involved and see if those bodies are there. If we can identify the other two, we may be able to decide who the third one was. Where's Krob, by the way?'

'Following Rezek. He's the only person in our team that Rezek hasn't seen. I sent him to follow Rezek after I dropped him at his house.'

'Good work, Navrátil. The person most likely to know who was in that grave before Adalheid Rezeková is her father, so let's follow him and see who he leads us to.'

Krob reported back by telephone.

'I followed General Rezek to the Prague City Archives in Chodovec, sir.'

'That figures,' Slonský replied. 'If he wanted to know whether the man in the grave had any children, the register of births would be the place to start. Did you ask who he asked about?'

'I asked, but they couldn't tell me. He used the online catalogue of births but he didn't ask for any particular birth certificate.'

'That only makes sense if the victim's name was so unusual that there could be no doubt about the father of the birth he looked up.'

'Or there were none to look up.'

'But if there weren't then we don't have a suspect for Adalheid Rezeková's killing.'

Krob, ever practical, brought them back to a key point. 'I don't want to appear half-hearted, sir, but I wondered if someone is going to relieve me.'

Slonský glanced at his watch. It was nearly seven o'clock in the evening. 'Yes. Or more exactly, no. You're stood down,

Krob. I'll think what to do next. Go home and I'll see you in the morning.'

Slonský grabbed his hat and coat and descended the stairs to the desk where Sergeant Salzer was on shift. 'Salzer, you've got children, haven't you?'

'A girl of fifteen, sir.'

'When you register the birth, what do you have to do?'

'You don't do much, sir. The hospital does it all and the registrar sends a birth certificate to the hospital. If you've already left then he sends it to your home, but usually you get it within a day or two.'

Slonský imagined a little light bulb bursting into life within his head. 'So the registrar must be given your home address in case he needs it?'

'I suppose so, sir.'

'Therefore, if an enquirer found a birth certificate in a certain name, he could get the address from a hospital?'

'In a small town he might, because there would only be one possible maternity hospital, but in Prague it wouldn't work. There are just too many options.'

Slonský thanked Salzer and continued into the street lost in thought. He would have put money on Rezek needing the birth certificate to be sure who the father was and where he lived, and yet Rezek hadn't bothered. Why not? Could it be that he was going to get someone else to do that for him? Had he spotted that Krob was following him? And why, Slonský wondered, was he wasting valuable drinking time thinking about work like this?

Chapter 9

Hanuš Himl was not a happy man. That is to say that he would not have planted the other flower beds if he had known that just a few days later a group of men with spades and sieves were going to dig them up again.

To his surprise Dr Novák proved to be very sympathetic to his feelings, and the diggers were instructed to lift off the top layer to a specified depth leaving it as undisturbed as possible, and to place it on plastic sheets he had set aside.

'There's no danger that we'll lose any evidence,' Novák explained to Slonský, 'given that Mr Himl must have dug this soil over several times over the years.'

Once the top layer had been removed from the flower beds, a team of technicians using ground penetrating radar moved in. Systematically they walked back and forth over the area of interest while Novák watched an image that was being compiled on a computer monitor.

'Can this really work?' Slonský asked.

'It's better when the bodies are new. It's been used following disasters to look for people under mud slicks, for example, but we may still get something, especially if the bodies are wrapped in a covering.'

Slonský peered at the screen. 'It just looks like a mess to me.'

'That's because you haven't been trained to interpret it.'

'So what do you see, then?'

'A mess. But it's not hopeless. Those flat sections are showing us that nothing has been disturbed, but there's an area that shows an anomaly.'

'An anomaly?'

'It's what we call a disturbance in the orderly layers of sub-soil. In other words, someone has been digging it up. Don't get excited; it may just be a drain or a cable. But this one is worth investigating, because it's nearly two metres long.'

'So a body could be within it?'

'Could be. There is something solid there.'

'How long before you send the men with the spades back in?'

'Let's finish the radar plot first. But you'll have to be patient, Slonský. They're going to be digging very slowly to ensure that they don't disturb any evidence. Why don't you go away for a while and I'll call you when we've finished?'

'I could have a little something to eat,' Slonský mused.

'Good idea.'

'Just to clarify, is this a coffee-and-pastry going away, or a sausage-and-potatoes followed by a piece of cake going away?'

'I've seen how fast you can put a couple of sausages away. We're talking hours, Slonský.'

'Ah. Right. I'll go and see what's been happening in the world of crime, then.'

'You do that.'

Krob was hanging around somewhere near Rezek's house just in case, but the rest of the team were in their offices when Slonský returned, so he suggested that they all decamp to the canteen where he could brief them on his discussions with Jelínek and Novák.

'Navrátil already knows this, because I spoke to him last night, but it seems possible that there are two other bodies in the grounds of the Red House,' Slonský told them once they were seated. 'I've just come from there where Dr Novák is doing something or other that lets him see under the ground.'

'And you're convinced that General Rezek knows who the original body was?' Peiperová pressed.

'No, but if he doesn't, I don't know who does.'

'We've gone through Adalheid's papers,' Peiperová continued, 'and they're not a lot of help. There was a diary entry blocking out Thursday morning, so perhaps she was expecting to be out late on Wednesday night, but not much more. Unopened post and food in the fridge that had passed its best before date.'

'Well, that's something. But if she had a night out, where did she go? We could try going round the restaurants and bars, but it'll take an age, even if we don't have a drink ourselves in each one.'

'We don't know for certain that she had that sort of a night out,' Navrátil insisted, 'so it would be hard to justify spending time on a door to door enquiry.'

'She was wearing very fancy underwear,' Slonský told him.

'All her underwear is like that,' said Jerneková. 'She's just given to exotic smalls.'

Slonský felt deflated. His case was crumbling, slowly but inexorably, and if it turned out that Rezek really did know nothing about the bodies in the Red House grounds, then that put the kybosh on his revenge theory. In which event, what alternative did he have?

Peiperová had a suggestion. 'Why don't we talk to her colleagues to see if any of them has any information that might throw some light on Adalheid's life? Eva Čechová told us Adalheid was meeting a man for dinner.'

'That's not necessarily a romantic dinner,' Navrátil remarked. 'It could just be a business meeting.'

'We need to clarify that,' Peiperová agreed. 'Did Eva just assume it was a romantic event, or had Adalheid said something to encourage that idea?'

'That sounds like a job for you and Jerneková,' agreed Slonský. 'Jerneková, did you find out anything about the car crash that killed Adalheid's husband?'

'It doesn't seem to have been reported to us, sir, at least not for any sort of investigation. We've got a formal note.' Jerneková consulted her notepad. '22nd April, 1986, sir. It was a Tuesday.'

Slonský seemed suddenly animated. 'When you say we've got a formal note, what do you mean?'

'It's logged in the event diary for the day, but there's no file opened.'

Slonský rubbed his hands together and evinced every appearance of glee. 'Splendid! At last we've got something!' Seeing the blank looks around the table, he felt compelled to elucidate. 'You don't understand what I'm getting at, do you?'

A variety of mumbled negatives and gently shaken heads displayed their puzzlement.

'This is where we could do with Krob. After his time with the city police, he would know what I'm on about. Walk it through with me. If this accident happened today, what would happen?'

'The crash would be reported to either the city police or to us, and whichever heard first would tell the other,' Navrátil answered.

'And that explains the log entry,' Slonský explained, 'because it would be entered as a notification at the moment it was received. That's straightforward. What happens next? Come on, Jerneková, you've just learned this!'

'Once we heard there was a fatality we'd call the ambulance service and the pathologist. The paramedics would verify that the person was dead, and then the pathologist would look into the circumstances. If he was suspicious he'd call us.'

'True,' Peiperová interjected, 'but we'd probably have picked it up anyway, because it could be some time before the pathologist could give an opinion. In real life, if the police officer and the pathologist agree that there's nothing suspicious, we'd close the case. If they didn't, we'd refer it to the prosecutor.'

'Ah! There you have it,' Slonský said. 'We'd open a file at the first report, then we'd add the pathologist's report, the investigating officer's report — if one was called out — and the prosecutor's decision to that file. At that point the file might be closed, but it would remain on file indefinitely so that if any questions were ever raised we could justify the decision. So the log entry exists because it is almost impossible to remove such an entry after the event without creating a huge amount of work renumbering everything since. That makes perfect sense. What is striking here is that there is no file corresponding to the original entry. None at all. Yet you've just demonstrated that there must once have been one.'

'Maybe it was just lost,' Navrátil suggested.

'And maybe it was stolen by the evidence pixies. But the most likely reason is that someone with high level access to files stuffed it up their jumper and walked out with it.'

'Even if that's true, how does it help us, sir?' Peiperová asked.

'Think who the victim was, lass.'

'We haven't got a name yet, sir.'

'No, we haven't. It would be a good idea if you found us one. But we know one key fact about him. Remember what

Vlk told us? "The son of a Deputy Minister of the Interior" was how he described Adalheid's husband. And that's exactly the sort of person who would have access to any file he wanted.'

'He stole the report into his own son's death?'

'No, Peiperová. But only a person with more clout than him could have done it with impunity. What would have happened in those days to someone who stopped a Party bigwig getting what he wanted?'

'That's an unfair question, sir,' Navrátil objected, 'because you're the only one who is old enough to remember that.'

'Good point,' Slonský conceded. 'Then I'll tell you a cautionary tale. When I was a young officer, there was a police driver of around my age. I forget his name, but it doesn't matter. One night he was driving round the city when a car came out of a side street at speed and crashed into his nearside rear wing. The driver of the other vehicle was the State Secretary for Heavy Industry, and he was full to the gills with vodka.

'Our man reported what happened. The next day he received a statement to sign in which it was alleged that he had reversed into the Secretary's car. He refused to do so and insisted that the Secretary was drunk. A few days later two fellows with heavy batons turned up and gave him the beating of a lifetime. He still refused to sign the statement, but they just forged his signature anyway. And it is my contention that if anyone had tried to suppress the enquiry into the death of the son of a senior Party figure, a similar thing would have happened, if the senior Party figure dared to arrange it.'

'But isn't it possible that his father knew that his son was responsible for his own death and ordered the file destroyed to protect his name?' asked Navrátil.

'No, because the father's best course would have been to keep the file but change the papers within it. The original pathologist's report saying the boy was drunk would have vanished and a new one would have been inserted saying it was just an unfortunate accident. So, I repeat my question: who has enough clout to get a file removed without consequences to himself? And to save you scratching your heads until you get splinters I'll give you the answer, courtesy of Sergeant Jelínek; the Deputy Head of Section 4 of the StB could have done it, otherwise known as General Rezek, because Section 4 investigated threats to state security and anything they decided was a threat could be destroyed.

'In fact, it wouldn't surprise me if Section 4 organised the accident. The only argument against that guess is that some public-spirited person bothered to report it, which suggests that the accident wasn't followed by sinister fellows in trench coats and dark hats telling people to forget what they'd seen. Remember that Vlk said that Adalheid was beaten by her husband. Can you imagine Rezek just standing by and letting that happen to his daughter? He'd let them separate but then he could take his revenge. I can imagine a couple of StB lads being sent out one evening to doctor the brakes on the husband's car while another one plied him with drink, including a Mickey Finn or two.'

'Could the StB really do that, sir?' Peiperová asked doubtfully.

'They could do whatever they wanted to do.'

'But what kind of people were they?' she continued.

'People like you and Navrátil.'

'Sir, I'd never be a party to anything like that,' protested Navrátil.

'Lad, you have the luxury of being able to say no. We didn't. You'd have been prime StB fodder. They've have snapped you up lickety-split.'

'Why, sir?'

'Because you've got brains and you speak a foreign language.'

'I don't understand, sir.'

'Navrátil, why do you think you were fast-tracked into the police service?'

'I don't know, sir. I've never stopped to ask.'

'Then I'll save you a job by telling you the answer. Historically, the Czech Republic scored very badly compared with other forces in terms of the educational achievements of its police. The quick way to fix that was to get some people with degrees in, hence your graduate entry scheme. Do you know that the StB never managed to fill its complement of officers? That was because to be an officer you had to have a certificate of completion of high school, and most of us didn't have it. You could be an ordinary StB oik without that, so they could have filled all those posts, but they were held back by not having enough officers to supervise them. And because there was a lot of competition for the lower posts, they could afford to be picky.

'In fact, there's some evidence that at one time the lower level personnel were better qualified than the officer caste. And the thing that they prized more than anything else was a gift for languages, because if you've going to eavesdrop on what foreigners are up to, you need an awful lot of people who speak foreign languages. You'd have had a really exciting job, lad, spending your days listening to English-speaking tourists telling their families what a wonderful time they've had and how great Czech beer is, and writing it all out longhand.'

'What possible interest is there in that, sir?'

'None at all, Navrátil, but if you don't listen to a lot of dross you don't get to hear the little pearl hidden in it.'

'So how come you weren't dragged into the StB, sir?' Jerneková asked.

'That's a very good question, and it's down to my foresight in being thick at school and trying very hard not to learn any languages. I mean, the only one I ever had to learn was Russian, and to me Russian always sounded a bit like drunk Czech, which is odd because most of the people I heard speaking it were drunk Russians. Anyway, I could never pass any exams in it. I had a narrow escape when I was in the Army and I didn't realise how low the pass mark was there, but fortunately I scraped under the bar by the skin of my teeth and kept up my record of complete failure. They'd have me in the ordinary police because they couldn't afford to be choosy, and since the StB and the police were basically one thing at the time I could have been transferred if I'd ever shown any promise, but I'm pleased to say I was a late developer. I also have to give credit to my wife, because her walking out on me sent me off to the bottle and ensured my performance levels were pitiful for the first half of the seventies. Back then, I was sucking Mrs Vodka's teat in a big way.'

'I can't drink vodka,' Jerneková confided. 'It makes me tearful.'

'Me too,' said Slonský.

Eva Čechová produced the requested key when Peiperová and Jerneková returned to visit her. 'I have to take it back personally, I'm afraid,' she said.

'That's not a problem,' Peiperová smiled. 'You can stay while we search Adalheid's desk if you like. We can talk while we do it.'

Eva nodded doubtfully. 'I didn't really know her that well,' she argued. 'Not socially. She's not one for girls' nights out. I mean...'

'We know what you mean. There's a bit of an age difference, isn't there?'

'Yes. And she could be quite cynical. On the other hand, I think she hoped that one day Prince Charming would come along.'

'When we last spoke, you said you thought Adalheid had a dinner date with a man.'

'Yes. But it was a bit odd. At first I thought it was a romantic thing, but then she was very matter of fact about it, so I wondered if it was something else.'

'She had a half-brother. Could it have been him?'

'I don't know. If she mentioned a name, I'm afraid I don't remember it.'

'Was there anyone here she was especially friendly with?'

'Maybe Barbora. They were about the same age, and I know they went to the opera together once or twice. She works in the finance department.'

'It would be really helpful if you could ask her if she could spare us a few minutes while we're here,' Peiperová said.

'In here?'

'Well, nobody else is going to be using this office, are they?' Jerneková replied.

Barbora was a woman in her mid-forties, and it took no time at all for Jerneková to decide that she was one of those irritating women who can just throw a headscarf on and immediately look good. The absence of a wedding ring marked her out as a woman who could spend her wages on herself, and a good chunk of her disposable income must have gone to her hairdresser. She wore black trousers, impeccably cut, an understated white blouse with a satin stripe and a gold cross and chain around her neck. Her shoes looked like ordinary loafers until you spotted the makers' name on a little plaque and realised that they came from the kind of store that Jerneková had never allowed herself to enter for fear that she would involuntarily part with all her worldly wealth in exchange for a handbag.

'How may I help?' Barbora asked. Even her grammar sounded expensive.

Peiperová introduced herself and Jerneková, and invited Barbora to sit, which the older woman did once she had selected the least stained chair in the room.

'We're trying to get some sort of idea who Adalheid Rezeková may have been meeting in the week that she disappeared,' Peiperová told her, 'but it seems that she was choosy who she shared personal information with. We heard that the two of you had some shared interests and wondered if you were able to help us.'

'If I could, of course I would want to, but I'm sure she never said anything to me about any men in her life.'

'It may not have been a romantic attachment,' Peiperová prompted.

Barbora frowned and appeared to be searching her memory. 'Did you know that Adalheid was once married?' she asked.

'So we understand.'

'It was not, it seems, a happy time for her, and it ended in divorce. Adalheid had rarely spoken of it to me until around a month ago, when I walked into this office and she was reading a letter. She had been crying.'

'The letter upset her,' concluded Jerneková.

'Perhaps, but I'm sure that her main feeling was one of anger. I asked her if something was wrong, and I thought she was going to tell me, but after a moment or two she folded the letter, threw it in the drawer of her desk, and said it was nothing important. We chatted about whatever it was I'd come to say to her, then as I was leaving she took the letter out again.'

'Can you tell us anything about it?' asked Jerneková.

'It was typed — or, at least, not handwritten. A standard piece of A4 paper folded into quarters, with only a line or two on the back. But the odd thing — dear me, you'll think I'm terribly inquisitive going on like this — was that it wasn't signed. It just ended in a line of typing.'

'An anonymous letter?' Jerneková asked.

'So it seemed. But it was clear that Adalheid didn't want to talk about it, so I let the matter drop. Then a few days later we went to a concert together and we were having a little supper at the Café Slavia beforehand. She seemed rather detached, and I asked her if she was quite well. She apologised and said that she was fine, just a little preoccupied, and then she said that she couldn't decide whether to let sleeping dogs lie. I asked in what sense, because that sort of sentence could mean anything or nothing, and she said that someone had been in touch with her asking if she wanted to know what really happened to her husband. I'd always understood that he was killed in some kind of accident, but she explained that they'd been divorced by then and when she heard of his death it hadn't provoked any sort of sympathetic feeling. I rather got the idea she'd expected something of that kind — he was fond of a drink or two, you see. But she said that it was one thing if he'd got drunk and driven into a wall and killed himself, and quite another if someone could prove that it hadn't been that way.

'She felt nothing for her ex-husband, but she had a kind heart and she would have hated an injustice done to anyone, so if there was some foul play involved, she would not have wanted to let it go unnoticed. Anyway, she asked me what I thought, and I said that it was hard to see why somebody should come forward after all this time. I gather she was a very young woman when he died. And — this is going to sound awful — I said that if someone wanted money from her for that information, I thought she should be very careful because I should doubt that it was genuine. But she said her informant didn't want money. He only wanted the truth to come out.' Barbora paused and sat back in her chair, having noticed that she had been creeping forward as she gave her account. 'Having said that, I don't know what Adalheid actually did about it, because she didn't confide in me any further on the matter.'

Slonský was beginning to doubt the value of keeping Krob hanging around in the rain near Rezek's house, because the old general had not set foot outside the door for a couple of days. This irritated the detective because, as his old mother had repeatedly said, if he was hanged for patience he'd die innocent.

Plainly Rezek had something in mind because he had asked to see the site. Then he had checked the register of births; or, more accurately, he had checked the index to the register. It all fitted. He was trying to work out who could have taken revenge on him by killing his daughter. The killer, whoever he or she was, had thrown down a challenge. Leaving Adalheid's body where he did was taunting Rezek, telling him "I can hurt you and you know why."

Slonský sipped his coffee as he dredged his memory for any similar cases during his career, but he could think of none quite like this. Revenge killings, yes, he'd had a few. There was the fellow in Karlín who had killed his wife's lover, severed the victim's penis and given it to her as a keepsake. And there was the man who had been defrauded of an inheritance by a lawyer and had waited in his office before stabbing him with his own paper knife. He could also bring to mind the occasional case of a murderer leaving the body in some sort of display. Discounting the black magic ritual type of killing, where display could hardly be avoided, he thought of the odd case of the poisoned woman left in her bed surrounded by rose petals, where the killer had taken the time to plait her hair. But revenge and display in the same killing was unusual.

Feeling sure that his brain was sluggish because his blood sugar level was low, Slonský returned to the counter for a refill and the stickiest pastry he could find. His hypothesis was supported by the sudden feeling he experienced as he stood in the queue to pay, the sense that things were becoming clearer and dropping into place. By the time Dumpy Anna took his money, he was feeling quite enlightened.

'You're looking very pleased with yourself,' she told Slonský.

'A smile is the natural result of seeing you,' he replied.

'Get away with you. You see me almost every day but you don't always smile.'

'I do, but inwardly. However, today I'm also smiling because an idea has come to me about a case I'm working on.'

'That's good.'

'Anna, if you were out for revenge on someone, how would you do it?'

'Is this a catch question? Are you going to pin something on me?'

'Not at all. I have a theory about the murderer's behaviour. Humour me.'

108

Anna rolled her sleeves up and straightened her white cap. 'I'd do what I do best. I'd cook them something special and put a suitable poison in it.'

'And then go home and wait?'

'Hell, no! Where's the fun in that? I'd want to watch them eat it. This is all make-believe, of course,' she added hurriedly.

Slonský smiled, collected his change, and playfully pushed her cap askew as he carried his tray away.

'Are you sure about this?' Navrátil asked as Slonský explained his idea an hour later.

'No, but I think it's a good bet. The killer's motive has nothing to do with Adalheid herself. He wants his revenge on Rezek, and I don't think it would satisfy him unless he knew that Rezek had spotted the lesson he was trying to teach.'

'So you think he's watching?'

'I'd be surprised if he wasn't. He wants to see Rezek squirm. The chances are that Krob hasn't been the only one watching Rezek's house.'

'Should I ask Krob to keep his eyes open for another watcher?'

'He's a bright lad. If he'd seen anyone hanging around, he'd have reported it off his own bat. And I guess the killer has seen what he wants to see by now. His job was done once the women turned up to give Rezek the news. He's got what he wanted. It's all square now.'

Navrátil was less certain. 'What makes you think being all square is good enough for our man?'

Slonský was taken aback. He had not considered this possibility. 'How do you mean?'

'Here you've got a man who has waited a long time — over thirty years — to take revenge. This is on the assumption that you're right about the murder of Adalheid Rezeková being all about revenge, which I'm not sure I completely buy just yet. Anyway, if someone has harboured that grudge for thirty years or more, why would he stop there? I wouldn't. If all he wanted was simple revenge, he'd kill Rezek. Why doesn't he do that? Because he wants Rezek to live on in misery. If you're right that the killer is a child of whoever was buried there first, then he wants Rezek to feel the pain of losing a close family member just like he experienced it. Plainly he can't kill Rezek's father, so he kills Rezek's child.'

'Why Adalheid? Why not Petr?'

'Because she was the favourite? Perhaps he didn't make the link between Petr and Rezek because Petr doesn't use the Rezek surname. Who knows? Whatever the reason, the one thing we can say is that it made perfect sense to him. This is not a random or spontaneous killer. He's planned this very carefully. And that brings me to two questions. One — having waited all this time, what spurred him into action now? And two, what's his next move?'

Slonský was in the grip of an unusual sensation, that of discovering that another policeman occasionally had a good idea. It had not taken him long after Navrátil's arrival to decide that this was a young man who could go right to the very top of the Czech police service, always provided that Slonský gave him suitable guidance and training, but he was taken aback that his fatherly counsel had produced results this quickly. Navrátil would not have spoken like this even six months earlier. Their relationship was changing and Slonský would need to keep on top of his game if he wanted to retain the upper hand in it.

'You think that something has triggered this?' he asked.

'I can't see why he would wait,' Navrátil replied. 'After all, Rezek is not a young man. He could have keeled over at any moment and deprived our killer of his victory. Something had to happen before our man could put his plot into effect, and the obvious thing is that he somehow discovered where his father was buried. Tricking Adalheid into meeting him, strangling her and dumping her body, he could have done any time. The one part of his plan he couldn't have done is leave the body somewhere that meant something to Rezek. It can only be recently that he has found out where those bodies were, and we can be pretty sure that Rezek didn't tell him. So who did?'

'Jelínek didn't know.'

'No, Jelínek told you he didn't know. Why would he admit anything?

'You're developing a very suspicious mind, young Navrátil.'

'If Jelínek said nothing, you'd keep badgering him. Better to let you have just enough that you'll go away. Maybe we need to ask him if anyone else has been asking any questions about the Red House.'

'Would he tell us?'

'He might if he thought he was in the frame as an accessory to the original killings. There's no statute of limitations on murder.'

'Not only are you becoming cynical, you're also developing a nice line in cunning. Well done, lad. Are you going to ask him, or am I?'

'You're the one who has met him before, sir. If he realises you weren't shaken off the scent he may let something else slip.'

'Good thought. Have you got any others?'

Navrátil walked over to the wall where the large map of Prague was hanging. 'Just one. I think our killer may live not far from Rezek.'

'Why do you say that?'

Navrátil took a couple of pins out of the box on the top of the filing cabinet. 'Here,' he began, inserting a yellow-headed pin, 'is Rezek's house. And here,' he continued while placing a red pin, 'is the depot where the electric cart was stolen.'

Slonský scratched his head. How had he missed that? 'How far apart are they?'

'Eight hundred metres? Say, a ten minute walk.'

'Maybe that's why Krob hasn't spotted anyone hanging around. He can watch from his own window.'

'It's possible. It may even be that he moved there so that he would be near to Rezek when the time came. But I can't imagine how anyone would know those carts were sitting there unless he'd walked or driven past, and I can't imagine why anyone would follow that road unless they were living locally. It's not on the way to anywhere.'

'Navrátil, you may be on to something. I insist that you let me buy you a celebration coffee and pastry.'

'You've just had one, sir.'

'Am I rationed? Come along.'

Slonský led the way from the room as Navrátil grabbed his jacket from the back of the chair and Slonský's wallet from his coat pocket. That was one of the first things he had learned. Just because Slonský invited you for a coffee, beer, sausage or anything else did not mean that he would have any way of paying when the bill came.

Dumpy Anna raised an inquisitive eyebrow. 'You again?'

'We're celebrating a moment of vital importance for the successful future of the Czech police service,' Slonský told her.

'You're retiring?' Anna asked.

'Have you been nobbled by Lieutenant Dvorník?'

'No, it was only my guess.'

'Well, it was wide of the mark. No, the cause for celebration is that the boy here has just come up with an idea all by himself.'

'I'm impressed. How long has he been with you?'

'Barely two years and already he's taking his first tentative steps towards being a top detective, under my tutelage, of course.'

'I'm glad he's not letting your help hold him back. I assume Lieutenant Navrátil is paying as usual?'

'No, I've got my wallet … ah.'

'Don't worry, sir. I liberated it from your pocket,' said Navrátil, offering the elderly leather object.

Slonský and Navrátil were having a relaxing time in the canteen when they spotted Sergeant Mucha on his way towards them with a concerned look on his face.

'I don't know why you don't just drag your desk down here and cut down on your walking,' Mucha grumbled.

Slonský looked around for other desks. 'Do you think they would let me?' he asked hopefully.

'Dr Novák is looking for you. He doesn't look too happy.'

'Novák never looks happy. It comes of spending all his time with stiffs. He must want for sparkling conversation — which, I suppose, is why he comes here.'

'Get off your backside and go and sparkle upstairs,' Mucha growled.

'You mean "Get off your backside and go and sparkle upstairs, sir,"' Slonský corrected him.

'If you insist. Just go.'

Slonský and Navrátil bounded upstairs and found their office empty, which puzzled Slonský until it dawned on him that Novák had probably made the mistake of going to Slonský's office on the assumption that he would be using it instead of slumming it with his juniors. Nudging the door open, he spotted the back of a familiar head.

'Dr Novák! I hope you haven't been waiting too long.'

'Around eleven minutes, but I wouldn't want to rush your coffee break.'

'Never mind, we're here now. What can I do for you?'

'I've brought my report on the triple burial.'

'So there were others?'

Novák polished his glasses before replying. He knew it irritated Slonský when he did that but he did not care. 'Two more, as described by your informant. They weren't evenly distributed. These two were separated by about a metre, the feet of A being above the head of B. I use the word "above" to mean further along the trench, not vertically over. The impression we saw the other day was about three metres from the middle one. It was also the other way round, lying feet to feet with its neighbour.'

'Any identifying features on these two?'

'No. Each was presumably naked when buried, and I've taken dental records though with so many fillings I'm not sure it will be conclusive for either.'

'I don't suppose you can suggest a cause of death either,' remarked Slonský glumly.

'Oddly enough, I can,' replied Novák. 'Each had a hole in the back of the head where a bullet went in and a bigger hole in the front where it came out.'

Slonský was rarely lost for words, but his jaw moved without any coherent sound being emitted.

'Am I to take it that this surprises you?' asked Novák.

'We were told that the only deaths at the Red House were people who died during questioning.'

'Perhaps they did, but they were assisted by a large lump of lead. Since they were probably shot indoors and the bullets passed right through, I don't have them, but these were not small wounds. I'd guess that they were nine millimetre bullets, standard issue in the Czech army and police thirty years ago.'

'I had a 7.62,' Slonský remarked.

'Yes, well, they'd hardly have given the likes of you one of the new ones, would they?'

'I counted myself lucky I had an actual gun instead of a piece of wood painted black,' Slonský admitted.

'Didn't you all have real guns?' Navrátil interrupted.

'Of course we did. What a scurrilous suggestion you make! As if the glorious Warsaw Pact would leave a fellow Pact member short of weapons, especially one that they had just invaded.'

Novák had opened the folder on his lap and was reading from his report. 'Body A was a man, probably in his late twenties or early thirties, but these things are very hard to judge precisely when you only have a skeleton to work with. He was around 178 centimetres tall. The best hope of identification may be that he was missing an adjoining pair of his upper right teeth, the canine and the first premolar. I don't think that happened post mortem because the sockets seem to have had time to repair. In a younger man the likeliest reason for someone to be missing those two teeth and only those two is an accident.'

Slonský was hurriedly making a pencilled note. 'What about Body B?'

'Here you have a slightly better chance. I'm going to guess that this man had been a basketball player, because he stood around 193 centimetres. We've also still got a bit of attached hair, showing that it was black with no sign of grey, and probably in his early thirties, give or take a couple of years. I've sent that hair for DNA testing.'

'So was Boy A bald, then?'

'No, but if hair isn't attached you can't assume that it came from the nearest body. There is some blonde hair there and I've taken a sample. We'll ask for DNA typing of both the hair and a bone sample and take it from there.'

'No bracelets or rings?'

'Unfortunately not, nor dog-tags or anything else with a name written on it. Nor can I tell you definitively that they were buried at the same time, though you have other evidence for that.'

Slonský nodded glumly. If only there was a registry somewhere of tall, dark men who hung around with medium-sized blond ones.

Chapter 10

Slonský had decided that if he did not buy a wedding present for Navrátil and Peiperová soon he might find that his workload stopped him shopping later, so he was engaged in research on the kind of thing that newlyweds might value. Realising that a female viewpoint could be useful he had ruled out asking his estranged wife Věra (too awkward), Peiperová (too involved), or his mother (too dead). Since Jerneková seemed not to have too high a view of marriage, this left him with either asking Major Lukas' wife and daughters, who would be terribly sensible about the whole thing, or Dumpy Anna in the catering department, who probably had a better idea of the available budget. Thus, it was that he slinked into the canteen having first peeked in to check that neither of the couple-to-be was lurking there.

'Have you got a minute?' he asked Anna.

'So long as you're not going to suggest a knee-trembler in the store room,' she answered, wiping her hands on her apron.

'Why would I do that?'

'I don't know, but one day my luck may change. What can I do for you?'

'I need some female advice.'

'If your hair thins any more, don't wear a combover,' Anna replied, and turned away as if her job was done.

'That wasn't it. And my hair isn't thinning. As it happens, I have the normal amount of hair. I just have an unusually big head.'

'I see. Well, what was it?'

'You know Navrátil and Peiperová are getting married soon?'

'How could I not? Every day I have to look at him goggling at her across the table with a face like a puppy that's been locked in a shed.'

'You've noticed that too, eh?'

'Talk about love's young dream. I mean, I'm very happy for them, and I hope they have a lovely life together, but I don't know what's going to happen once he realises that she doesn't have wings and a halo.'

'It was toilet paper that did for me,' Slonský reminisced.

'What do women do with so much toilet paper?'

'It's part of our glorious mystery,' Anna revealed. 'A secret never to be shared with men.'

'Evidently not. So, the thing is, I need to get them a wedding present, and I have no idea what the usual thing is.'

'If you'll take my advice,' Anna confided, 'the usual thing is rubbish. It's something they'll never use, like an egg boiler or a fondue set. What they need is a good boot scraper.'

'That's more along the lines I had in mind,' Slonský admitted, 'but I'd like something that's going to last their whole married life.'

'A cast iron boot scraper will last for decades,' she persisted.

Slonský walked over to where Jerneková was sitting at her desk attacking a carton of yoghurt with gusto.

'Are you alone?' Slonský whispered.

Jerneková looked around her. There was nowhere that a person more than thirty centimetres tall could possibly be concealed. 'So far as I know,' she answered.

'Good,' Slonský continued. 'Have you decided what you're getting Navrátil and Peiperová as a wedding present?'

'Yes,' Jerneková said confidently, and returned to licking the back of her spoon.

'What is it?'

'Nothing.'

'Nothing?'

'That's what Kristýna said they wanted off me. Nothing.'

'Yes, she says that, lass, but it doesn't mean she actually wants nothing.'

Jerneková frowned. 'It sounds like it to me. If she wanted something she only had to say so, but when I asked she said nothing. And she's a truthful girl, so I took her at her word.'

'She hasn't said she wants nothing to me,' said Slonský doubtfully.

'Then she probably wants something off you, sir,' Jerneková continued, and snapped the top off her banana in a marked manner.

Slonský lobbed his hat on the countertop, his standard method of conveying that a discussion was needed.

Mucha summoned an officer to stand by the large register in which all events and discussions of an official nature must be logged, and suggested with an inclination of his head that Slonský might wish to come to the side of the front desk.

'I was hoping,' confided Slonský, 'that female colleagues in this building would assist me with my enquiries, but so far they have been a complete washout.'

'I trust,' murmured Mucha, 'that in this case "enquiries" is not a euphemism for goings-on in the evidence room?'

'God, no,' sighed Slonský. 'I couldn't be bothered with that. No, what I was — hang on, who was doing that in the evidence room?'

'My lips are sealed,' said Mucha. 'Wild horses wouldn't drag Strausz's name out of me.'

'Strausz? He was...?'

119

'Regularly.'

'With those teeth?'

'Apparently it didn't put women off. And being able to eat an apple between the bars of a cell is quite a party trick when you think about it.'

'Even so, you'd think women would have more self-respect.'

'It wasn't like it was all the women. No more than three at the outside.'

'Jesus Maria!' Slonský tried to return to his original line of questioning but found that an image of former Lieutenant Strausz and three compliant policewomen had somehow intruded itself into his head and refused to leave. There was a long silence, at least by Slonský's standards.

'You wanted something,' Mucha prompted.

'Eh? Oh, yes. Sorry — Strausz put it out of my mind. I'm trying to get an idea for a wedding present for young Navrátil and Peiperová, but nobody I've asked has had anything useful to suggest. What are you getting them?'

'I don't know. I was going to ask you. What's your current favourite?'

'Dumpy Anna suggested a good boot scraper.'

'Always practical,' said Mucha. 'Saves your rugs getting spoiled.'

'It's not very romantic, though, is it?'

'You old softie. There's more to life than romance, you know.'

'Don't I know it. And in my case it's just as well.'

Mucha pushed himself up off his elbows. 'Well, I can't stand gabbing to you all day. In the next twelve minutes I've got to give a sandwich to a couple of housebreakers Dvorník has in cells six and seven.'

'Good for Dvorník. What's on the menu today?'

'I like to keep it simple. You have to think of allergies and all that, so I go for lettuce with no mayonnaise.'

'That'll teach them. One of those every six hours and they'll soon be begging to confess. Do you want me to save you the walk and fetch them for you?'

'No need,' said Mucha, producing two parcels from under the counter. 'I get them when the six hours clock starts ticking, then they're beginning to stale nicely when they're due.'

'How thoughtful. Anyone I know?'

'Almost certainly. Don't you know all the housebreakers in Prague?'

At which point an idea came to Slonský.

Valentin was sitting in his usual alcove with the newspaper spread out in front of him when he realised Slonský was casting a large shadow across the page.

'Forgive me for broadcasting your shame to the world,' said the detective, 'but isn't that a tomato juice you're drinking?'

'With a dash of tabasco in it,' Valentin indignantly replied. 'I'm not a wimp.'

'Even so, why are choosing to imbibe a so-called drink made from squashed vegetables?'

'I think tomatoes are technically fruits, Josef.'

'Stop evading the point.'

'It's simple. I'm still on that detoxing programme to spare my liver, so I have two days a week when I drink no alcohol. Or is it meant to be five?'

'I bet those two feel like five.'

'You may be right, Josef. Anyway, I've had to cut back on the sparkling water. It was playing merry hell with my insides. I've got more wind than the Prague Philharmonic.'

'Maybe I'll sit somewhere else. Like outside.'

'No need. It's okay so long as I stick to this stuff.'

'Good. I'll get you a top-up,' Slonský told him. 'I need to borrow what's left of your brain.'

'For a very old friend you can be incredibly rude sometimes, you know?'

'That's what old friends are for. Like my dear granny used to say, a bit of plain speaking never hurt anyone. Now, are you sitting comfortably?'

'Yes, thank you.' Valentin raised his glass in a toast. 'Your very good health.'

'And yours,' Slonský replied. 'I hope that stuff makes a difference because I'd hate to find a good mate had been drinking that muck and he still pegged out on schedule.'

They sat in companionable silence for a moment or two before Slonský spoke again.

'I bet I'm enjoying this beer more than you're enjoying that.'

'Goes without saying. But you know the expression — my body is a temple.'

'In ruins?'

'If you're going to pick on me all night —' Valentin began.

'Truce!' Slonský said quickly. 'I've actually come to ask your help.'

'Really? Ask away, then.'

'Do you know any local dissidents? I don't mean today, I mean the fellows from the sixties and seventies.'

Valentin scratched his beard. 'The big name ones are mainly dead, I think. What do you want them for?'

'I need to identify three bodies, and I think they're likely to have been dissidents around 1970.'

'Three? I thought you'd found one?'

'Dug up another two.'

'Why don't you just flatten the Red House and dig the whole garden up?'

'I don't think the powers that be will let me do that.'

'Shame. I'd be prepared to lend a hand to see the back of that place.'

Slonský's stomach was rumbling, so he paused to organise a little something to fill the hole. 'Do you want anything to eat?' he asked Valentin.

'No, thanks. I don't want to spoil my dinner.'

'Neither do I. That's why I'm only having a couple of sausages.'

'Very abstemious of you.'

Slonský ignored the barb and returned to contemplation of the alluring contents of his glass. 'The thing is, old friend, we've got very sketchy details of the two whose bodies we have, and no description at all of who the third one was. I thought that if we could find someone who can put possible names to the first pair based on those descriptions, he may also be able to guess who the third one was likely to have been, based on known associations.'

'It's worth a try,' Valentin conceded. 'But wouldn't three people going missing at once have attracted some notice, even in 1970?'

'You'd think so, but not necessarily. Let's take a hypothetical example. Suppose that you and I were dissidents then. For reasons of basic security, however much we trusted each other we'd tell each other as little of our plans as we could because you just don't know who your real friends are in a totalitarian state.'

'You can bet I'd have told you nothing,' Valentin agreed.

'And I'd have reciprocated. So if I disappear, what will you do? First, you may not notice for a while, but if you do you won't want to bring the attention of the authorities to the fact that I may have done a runner. You'd want to find me yourself rather than invite the security police to investigate us. So it would be a while before you conclude that I really have gone; and even then, you don't know if that's a good or a bad thing. Maybe if I get to the West I'll send you a postcard, but I might not, especially if I'm paranoid about the StB coming to get me wherever I am, so you have every reason to keep quiet. The only time when you might feel it was worth making a noise about it all would be if you knew I was in custody, when you'd want to attract public support, especially in the West.'

'I can follow all that,' Valentin decided. 'So your idea is that probably people knew these three had vanished, but didn't want to make a fuss about it in case they'd escaped somewhere?'

'It's possible.'

'It's possible if their friends believed that's what they had in mind. Do we know any more?'

'Jelínek said that he understood that the three were arrested because they'd been trying to lobby the West German government to stop supporting the East Germans. Does that make sense to you?'

Valentin took out his phone. 'No, but I know who can tell us.' He spoke briefly to someone and broke off the call to tell Slonský that Dr Bitt would join them as soon as he could get there.

'Who's Dr Bitt?' Slonský asked.

'He's a teacher of some sort at the university. Lecturer, Professor, I can't remember. Anyway, he specialises in the Cold War era.'

When the door opened and Bitt entered, Slonský could barely disguise his surprise. He had expected that Bitt, like most professors he had met, to be wizened and elderly, whereas Bitt looked not much older than Navrátil. He wore a hiking jacket and it was uncertain whether he had started shaving yet. His eyes finally lit upon Valentin, who effected introductions. To Slonský's delight, Bitt requested a beer and expressed concern that Valentin was reduced to drinking tomato juice.

'It's got tabasco in it,' Valentin grumbled.

'He's not a wimp,' Slonský explained.

'I'd be more convinced if he drank a bottle of tabasco with a splash of tomato in it,' Bitt pronounced.

At Valentin's invitation Slonský repeated the information he had to Bitt.

'Any thoughts?' he asked.

'It all rings true,' Bitt declared. 'The key to this is Willy Brandt.'

'That German politician?' Slonský confirmed.

'That's the fellow,' Bitt replied. 'He had been Mayor of Berlin for over a decade when he became Chancellor of West Germany in 1969, and he proposed a very different way of dealing with the East. Instead of out-arming them, he planned to seduce them.'

'What — all of them?' Slonský asked incredulously.

'I was speaking figuratively,' Bitt told him. 'Brandt had presided over the reconstruction of West Berlin. In West Germany the economy was whizzing along and the difference in the standard of living between West and East was widening all the time, but of course the East did not know that because most of us could not go there. Brandt's idea was that the West should support the East with grants and credits to enhance trade. If it worked, the regimes in the Soviet bloc would become less threatened and would defuse the military situation, but that trade would also mean that ordinary citizens in the East would see how different things were under capitalism and would want the same thing themselves. Thus the international tension would be replaced by internal tension.'

'And what was the reaction to his plan?' Slonský demanded.

'Mixed, as you might expect,' Bitt replied. 'The East took some time to warm to it, but it went down very badly with dissidents over here. Remember that just the previous year we'd had Warsaw Pact troops marching around Prague, and there were still some stationed on our territory. The dissidents thought that going soft on East Germany would make it much less likely that there would be reform in the Eastern bloc. They may have been right.'

'But why did the authorities here want to stop dissidents giving West Germany a hard time?' Slonský persisted.

'Because in August 1970 Brandt signed the Treaty of Moscow, which recognised the existing borders of countries across the Eastern bloc. In effect he was recognising all those countries. Bear in mind he had to start with the USSR because that was the only Warsaw Pact country that West Germany had diplomatic relations with. So with that Treaty the Russians had achieved a major aim of their foreign policy, with the promise of more to come. The last thing they wanted was for some high-minded patriots to try to stop Brandt.'

Slonský took another mouthful of his beer and thought hard. 'We've got the bodies of two men who we think were arrested by the Security Service, imprisoned at the Red House and subsequently executed there. Do you have any idea how we could identify them?'

To his credit, Bitt took the question seriously. 'I am assuming that in asking me this you have already decided that forensic techniques are unlikely to supply you with an answer?' he asked.

'Only if we're very lucky,' Slonský replied. 'There's a chance that comparing dental records may do it, but it would be much, much easier if we had a small list of names, then we may be able to confirm an identification with dental records.'

'Is there reason to think that the two disappeared at the same time?'

'It's very likely. An eye-witness describes their graves being prepared simultaneously and they were buried together.'

Bitt drained his glass and caught the eye of a waiter. 'Another of those, please, and a refill for these two gentlemen.'

The waiter gingerly picked up Valentin's glass and inspected it.

'What is it, sir?'

'Tomato juice with a dash of tabasco.'

'He's proving he's not a wimp,' Slonský added helpfully.

'Do you have any information you can share with me?' Bitt asked when the waiter had left.

Slonský drew out his notebook and flipped it to the correct page. 'The first man was late twenties or early thirties, and around 178 centimetres tall. He was missing two teeth in his upper right jaw. The second one was much taller, around 193 centimetres with black hair. He was probably in his early thirties.'

'193 centimetres. Great — he's the one they'll remember, then.' Bitt checked his watch. 'It's not too late. There's no time like the present, if you're prepared to sacrifice your bacchanalian pleasures.'

Valentin folded his arms pointedly. 'I don't like the way you looked at me when you said that,' he groused.

Bitt turned to Slonský and grinned. 'It would be a friendly gesture if we took a bottle of something to keep the cold out,' he suggested.

'It's quite warm for the time of year,' Slonský argued.

'Yes, but if you're an old man in an old flat and you can't afford heating, a bottle is a great comfort.'

'Caught your drift,' said Slonský, and bought a bottle of schnapps at a store as they went past. He wiggled the bag so Valentin could hear clinking. 'Don't worry, I got you a bottle of tomato juice so you won't feel left out. And that tabasco stuff.'

On the way Bitt explained some of the history of their host.

'Karel Matoušek was never in the first rank of the dissidents, not one of those the foreign press lauded, but he should have been. He didn't speak any foreign languages and he wasn't one for public speaking. But he did some great work in the factories around Prague explaining to the workers that the dissidents were not American stooges, and he could say that because he knew them all. When the regime was trying to pass the dissidents off as a bunch of unworldly intellectuals, Matoušek was a one-man demonstration that it wasn't so. After the Velvet Revolution, he just walked away and got on with his life. He had no wish to be part of the power elite, so he put his overalls back on and went back to his old job fixing elevators and hoists. If he takes to you, he's a mine of information. He's helped me a lot over the years.'

They rounded the corner and Bitt stopped walking while he looked up at the windows. 'The light is still on. One tip, if I may. Matoušek takes his time answering. Don't rush him — he'll get there in the end. If anyone knows who your men are, I'd be pretty sure it's Matoušek.'

They climbed a couple of flights of stairs and Bitt rapped on the door. They could hear shuffling, and finally the door was opened to reveal a small, sturdy man in his eighties. He wore stained brown trousers and at least two sweaters, the collars of which were contending for the front position, and thick woollen socks.

'Dr Bitt!' he croaked. 'Good to see you.' He pumped the academic's hand furiously then looked up at Slonský.

'Slonský, Josef,' the detective announced, 'and this is my friend Mr Valentin.'

'I'm helping them with some research,' Bitt explained, 'and I think we need your invaluable memory again.'

'You'd better come in,' said the old man. 'Sorry about the voice — I go days without speaking to a living soul, then when I need to talk it won't work.'

Bitt clapped him on the shoulder and assured him that they could understand him perfectly.

Once in the front room, Slonský produced his bottles and Bitt collected together some tumblers so Slonský could pour. They toasted Matoušek's continued good health and each took a slug, which resulted in Valentin coughing furiously until he finally regained the power of speech.

'What in hell's name is that?' he gasped.

'Tomato juice,' said Slonský.

'What else?'

'Tabasco,' claimed Slonský. 'That's what it says, anyway.'

'Give it here!' Valentin demanded. Rotating the bottle so that he could inspect the label closely he held it under the dim central light bulb. 'Nowhere on there do I see the word tabasco,' he snarled.

'Of course not,' Slonský replied. 'It's in Vietnamese.'

'Aren't those chilli seeds floating in it?'

'Possibly,' conceded Slonský.

'I'm no linguist, Slonský, but I reckon it's a fair bet that the Vietnamese word "Jalapeño" that appears on the label translates into Czech as "Jalapeño", don't you think?'

'I guess you're on sound ground there,' Slonský admitted. Their attention was drawn to Matoušek, who was rolling around his chair in laughter.

'This pair are like Laurel and Hardy,' he said to Bitt. 'Did you bring them to cheer me up? What else do they do?'

'The big one is a police officer,' explained Bitt, 'while the little one is a top investigative journalist.'

Matoušek's eyebrows arched. 'You don't say? Well, he investigated the contents of that bottle pretty quickly.' He broke into a renewed fit of giggles.

Bitt gestured to the others to resume their seats. 'Well, now that we've broken the ice, so to speak, let me explain what they want to know. Two bodies have been found in the grounds of the Red House.'

Matoušek instantly stopped laughing. 'The Red House?' he murmured. 'Is that still running?'

'It's a teacher training college now,' Slonský explained, 'but we think these bodies probably date from 1970 or thereabouts. Each had been shot. Obviously we want to put a name to them, but we don't know where to start.'

Bitt picked up the story. 'There isn't a lot to go on, but the pathologists have come up with some basic details.' He nodded to Slonský to take over.

'One was in his late twenties or early thirties, and around 178 centimetres tall. The best identifying feature is that he was missing two adjacent teeth in his upper right jaw. The other one was taller, around 193 centimetres. He was probably in his early thirties and had black hair.'

Matoušek chewed his thumb. 'Around 1970, you say?'

'So it seems,' Slonský replied.

'One metre ninety-three,' Matoušek mumbled. 'He ought to be easy to remember.'

As instructed by Bitt, they sat patiently while Matoušek mulled over his memories. Finally they could see him knotting his brow and he rapped three or four times on his forehead with his knuckle as if trying to make his brain change gear.

'Bartek!' he announced. 'Michal Bartek. He was a half decent basketball player but his left hand wasn't much good.'

'You mean it was malformed?' asked Slonský.

'Not that I know of. He just couldn't shoot with it. He'd never have made it at the top level because defenders knew if they forced him to go to the left he probably wouldn't score.'

'And nobody noticed he was missing?'

'If I remember correctly, he'd spoken about trying to get to the West to see if he could get a professional contract. I don't think he was star-struck — he was too old for that — but it might have kept the wolf from the door while he sorted out something else to live on.'

'So if the taller one was Bartek, who might the shorter one be?'

Matoušek shook his head. 'Almost anyone. He didn't have a best mate he always hung around with.'

'According to our information,' Slonský persisted, 'they were picked up by the StB because they were planning to go to West Germany to try to persuade the government to stop being friendly to the East Germans. Who would have asked them to do that?'

Matoušek looked doubtful. 'I don't recall that ever being a plan that we had as a movement,' he said. 'More likely a scheme they cooked up themselves.' He tapped Bitt on the forearm. 'Do you know Martin Fischer?' he asked.

'Slightly.'

'If anyone would know, he would. Fischer was brought up German-speaking and had contacts there. I'd lay you a crown to a halér that if there was such a notion around, Fischer would have been in on it.'

'Do you know his address?' Bitt asked.

'No,' said Matoušek, 'but he used to drink at the Silver Lion. Do you know it?'

'Yes!' Slonský and Valentin barked together.

They left the remainder of the schnapps — not to mention the Vietnamese hot sauce — at Matoušek's flat, and strode out towards the Silver Lion, which was an old spit and sawdust bar in a side street with a very localised customer base. Tourists rarely went there, and if they did they didn't return, because any kind of novelty — such as an unfamiliar face — was likely to attract attention there. Fortunately Slonský had dropped in often enough over the years not to be completely unknown, so when he asked the barman if Mr Fischer was in the place the man stopped polishing a glass for long enough to point to a heavy-set man who was playing chess near the stove.

Slonský, Bitt and Valentin sat themselves down as close as they could get, which was at the table by the window. All that could be seen through the glass was the bar's backyard, which was covered in litter, but the effect was attenuated by the thoughtfulness of the staff who had ensured that you could barely see through the disgusting windows.

Valentin weakened and ordered a beer.

'Do you want tabasco in it?' Slonský asked him.

'Why the hell would I want tabasco in it?' Valentin demanded, while the barman simply added the idea to his list of fancy city centre perversions that wouldn't be introduced into his bar.

Slonský had not played chess for a long time, but even he could see that Fischer had the upper hand in the battle before them. He knew enough to know that two of those castle things were worth more than a castle and a horse, especially when they were side by side and causing mayhem right down the middle of the board. It wasn't long before Fischer's opponent extended his hand and acknowledged his defeat.

Fischer dabbed his ample brow with an improbably large handkerchief and glanced at the clock. He looked as if he was thinking of leaving, so Slonský quickly introduced himself and asked if he could have a word. Fischer agreed and waddled over to join them. By good fortune there was just enough space for his ample frame if he squashed Valentin against the wall, so that was what he did.

Bitt explained that they had just been to see Matoušek who had, in turn, directed them to Fischer. Slonský described the discovery of the bodies and gave the limited description that he had.

'The story that has been suggested to us,' he said, 'is that Bartek and two others were arrested by the StB in 1970 because they had been attempting to persuade West Germany to reverse its new policy of aiding the Eastern bloc, but we don't know that such an attempt was ever made. Mr Matoušek thought that if anyone would know of such a plot, you would.'

Fischer sipped at a glass of something expensive and herbal. Slonský had never taken to these mysterious concoctions of herbs and could not understand the popularity of drinks which, in his eyes, consisted of a compost heap in a glass.

'Mr Matoušek is overstating my prominence,' Fischer declared, his voice slurred by age, a few drinks and a lot of surplus skin around his neck and jaw. 'But I did know Bartek. He was not a stupid man. He reasoned that Brandt's policy might work in the long run, especially if we behind the Wall became dependent on the handouts and could not cope if they were suddenly withdrawn, but it would take a decade or more and ruin the lives of a generation of Czechs. Bartek's idea was rather different. Do you know the story of Trakia Plovdiv's football match in the English city of Coventry?'

His question drew blank looks all around, so Fischer continued.

'I think it was a little after the events you describe, but it illustrates Bartek's point well. The Bulgarian players travelled to Coventry and were given some time to shop and buy souvenirs. And that is what they did, but the souvenir they wanted was English wallpaper. You couldn't get it in Plovdiv, apparently, and what they did not use themselves they were able to sell at a handsome profit. This was just another in a long line of Eastern bloc sports teams going to the West and bringing back consumer goods that were unobtainable at home. Bartek had himself travelled with a basketball team to Munich and he firmly believed that if Czechs saw for themselves the standard of living that ordinary people in the West had it would spur public unrest and ultimately regime change.

'Bartek knew that the Eastern bloc would not simply allow its citizens to travel freely abroad, but he thought if the West fostered educational, sporting and cultural exchanges it would chip away at this lack of freedom. An orchestra travelling to France, for example, would mean a hundred people exposed to Western values. Of course, just as he was sceptical about Brandt's Ostpolitik so others were doubtful about his plan. Until, that is, he had the chance to put it into effect.'

Fischer took another sip.

'One of our top basketball clubs was very successful in a European tournament and Bartek was part of the backroom staff. He certainly wasn't a player for them; I suspect he looked after their kit or some such duty. At any event, he travelled with them on their away trips to the West and saw for himself how affected the players were by what they thought was rampant luxury. I think the other man whose body you have may have been called Toms — Vlastimil Toms, I think — who was another of the coaching staff at the club. Toms had an injury caused by an elbow in the mouth during a particularly fraternal match in Moscow, if my memory suffices. Those encounters were always rough affairs. I thank God I haven't a sporting bone in my body. Nobody ever lost two teeth playing chess.'

Slonský was making notes as quickly as he could. 'Thank you, Mr Fischer,' he responded. 'We'll certainly follow this up. The problem is really with the third man, but of course we don't have a body for that one. Do you have any idea who that might be?'

'I'm afraid I haven't,' Fischer answered. 'But all is not lost. To the best of my knowledge, Bartek's wife is still alive. I've no idea where she lives, I'm afraid, but I'm sure the police have ways of finding that out for themselves.' Slonský closed his book and was about to thank Fischer when the latter continued.

'At least, they always had in my day, and I suppose things to be no different now, more's the pity.'

Chapter 11

The following morning found Slonský in his office, which is to say the office that had previously been Captain Lukas's, because Slonský also maintained a desk in his old office (now the domain of Navrátil and Krob) and, in order to appear even-handed, in the office that was now primarily used by Peiperová and Jerneková. Slonský was busy adjusting the position of his chair until it was in just the right place to allow him to put his feet on his desk without difficulty.

'You look very comfortable here,' said a voice.

Glancing up, Slonský realised that the speaker was Lukas himself, and attempted to lurch to his feet respectfully.

'Don't get up, please!' Lukas insisted. 'And I hope you'll forgive the intrusion.' He peeked into the corridor and shut the door to the office. 'I am here on a mission for my wife.'

'Really, sir?'

'She has been looking for a wedding present for the two young officers and has settled on a set of bed linen, but she just wanted me to check that nobody else had the same idea.'

Slonský was not quite sure what "bed linen" was, but felt that the answer was obvious. 'I think Mrs Lukasová need have no concerns, sir. I don't know anyone else planning such a thoughtful gift.'

'That's a relief, I don't mind telling you. The hours we've spent discussing this... Do you mind if I sit down?'

'It's your office, sir.'

'No, it's your office now.'

'It'll always be your office in my eyes, sir.'

'I can't have two, Slonský, and I have one in the other wing now.'

Slonský could see no good reason why an officer couldn't have as many offices as he could lay his hands on, but he decided to let the matter drop.

'How are things coming along?' Lukas asked.

'We've got a particularly troubling murder on our hands. A woman who worked at the university who was killed and buried in the grounds of the Red House.'

'What an extraordinary place to bury her! Do you think that's significant?'

'At last — someone else thinks the same way as I do. Yes, it seems to me highly significant. And what's more, she was buried in a grave in which there had previously been another body. When our murderer deposited Adalheid Rezeková he collected whoever was there before.'

Lukas had always been good at displaying his amazement, and he did so now, by letting his jaw drop and pumping it ineffectually a couple of times without issuing any noise. 'That must have been a considerable undertaking,' he finally managed to say. 'He took a great risk in staying there long enough to do that. How can he have known that he wouldn't be disturbed?'

'Maybe he just took his chance, but it's a good question. It's a teacher training college now, so if they have security at all it's probably just an old man sitting in the foyer.'

'So I suppose your assumption is that there was a link between the murderer and the first body?'

'It seems logical. In which event the motive is simple revenge, because the second victim was the daughter of a high-ranking StB officer.'

'Rezek, Rezek,' Lukas repeated to himself. 'Klement Rezek?'

'That's the one.'

'Is he still alive? I guess he must be, or the revenge would be pointless.'

'Very much so. Alive and kicking.'

'If he's kicking, he hasn't changed,' Lukas replied. 'He was one of the nastiest people I've ever encountered.'

'I didn't know you'd met him.'

'He was a deputy section head in the security service when I was first nominated for promotion. In those days you had to be interviewed to verify your political reliability before promotion was confirmed. I regret that I was found insufficiently zealous and my promotion was withheld.'

'By Rezek?'

'I don't know how far he was involved, but by his directorate.'

'Maybe I ought to add you to my list of suspects, sir.'

'Do you have many?'

'Yours would be the only name on it at present. But we've discovered that two other bodies were buried at the same time. We've provisionally identified them as men called Bartek and Toms, dissidents who disappeared in 1970. Each had been shot in the back of the head.'

'Presumably there is no report on these events in the files, or the team who have been trawling through the StB records would have charged someone with the murders.'

'But if Rezek pulled the trigger he won't have dirtied his hands digging the graves. Somebody must know about that. Whether they're alive or not is another matter.'

Lukas stood and straightened his uniform. 'Captain Bendík may know of some way we can find out who was stationed there then. I'm not promising anything, but there is a lot of old

StB material that hasn't yet been catalogued. He has some contacts there.'

'That would be very helpful, sir.'

Lukas left the room, and once again Slonský asked himself whether someone who retired and then came back to work was morally obliged to return his retirement present.

Krob had been given the morning off to go with his wife for an antenatal appointment, so it was quite a surprise for Slonský when he turned up for work at half past eleven. Slonský could think of no other policeman who would have reported for duty when he had been given time off. Except perhaps Navrátil. And maybe Peiperová. And, of course, Mucha, if his sister-in-law invited herself for a visit. Come to think of it, Slonský had done it himself in the past, largely out of boredom.

Krob knocked on Slonský's open door and entered upon command.

'Have you got a moment, sir?'

'Of course. Everything okay at the clinic?'

'Yes, thank you. But that's not what I wanted to ask about. I've made a mistake.'

Slonský tapped the side of his head sharply to check his ears were working correctly. He had rarely, if ever, heard a policeman confess that. 'What kind of mistake? Is this something I'm going to have to report up the line?'

'No, nothing like that, sir. I made an assumption and it occurs to me that it was wrong.'

'You intrigue me. Speak on, fair youth.'

'You remember that I followed General Rezek to the registry of births, sir?'

'Yes. He looked at the catalogue but didn't ask for any particular birth certificate.'

'He didn't need to, sir.'

'No?'

'No, sir. It came to me while I was sitting in the waiting room this morning. Any child of the three men must have been alive when they were killed. And Rezek would have known of them. Assuming he knew which of the three had been dug up, he'd know whose children were likely to be responsible. And he already knew their names. I think he was just refreshing his mind. He knows the surname, and perhaps the child's age, so the index would give him the first name. He doesn't need anything else.'

Slonský slapped his hand loudly on the top of his desk. 'Damn! I missed that. Of course he doesn't. But somehow he has to find the address of the man he's after.'

'There are plenty of ways to do that, especially if it's not a common name. Perhaps the phone book, or he still has contacts in the police.'

'Anyone who knew Rezek when he was still working has to be fifty or over. But it's just about possible. Perhaps OII can flush out anyone who has been sharing that information?'

'I don't think anyone has, sir.'

'Why do you say that?'

'Because Rezek hasn't done anything. I can't imagine that if he knew where to find the killer of his daughter he'd do nothing about it.'

'Good point. But we can't afford to wait for that to happen. We have to get there first or someone else is going to end up dead. Admittedly they'll be a murderer, but if we're going to let murderers and victims sort these things out themselves we may as well restrict ourselves to issuing parking tickets.'

Peiperová too had been reviewing the information that she had collected, but rather than take it straight to Slonský she was sitting opposite Jerneková in the canteen.

'I've been thinking about our chat with Barbora,' she said.

'Me too,' Jerneková replied.

'What were you thinking about?'

'I was thinking that Barbora isn't telling us everything. Obviously the killer couldn't murder Adalheid by letter, so they must have met up. Since Barbora had been told everything else, why wouldn't she be told about a meeting?'

'I wondered about that too,' admitted Peiperová, 'but what if she wasn't told because she couldn't be?'

'How do you mean, couldn't be?'

'If she was away, for example. Or there was too short a time between the appointment being made and it being kept.'

'But Adalheid would have the choice of appointment.'

'Suppose the killer says he has the information but he's about to go away for a prolonged time,' Peiperová suggested. 'They have to meet that evening.'

'Then he's a liar, because we know he put her in the freezer so he didn't go away.'

'Yes, but if you go killing innocent women thirty years after someone dear to you was killed, telling a fib isn't going to hold you back.'

'Fair point,' Jerneková conceded.

'If you were going to meet a strange man you hadn't met before, what would you do to keep safe?' Peiperová asked.

'I'd keep a kitchen knife in my handbag.'

'Beyond that, let's say.'

Jerneková considered. 'I'd meet in a very public place.'

'They're going to talk about something they won't want overheard, so perhaps that isn't as easy as she'd like.'

'They can whisper. I'd still pick a public place.'

'I went back to the post-mortem results on Adalheid. She hadn't eaten for a few hours before she died, so it wasn't a dinner date.'

'Liquid dinner. I've had a few of those,' Jerneková sighed.

'You think they met in a bar?'

'Obvious place. Lots of noise to hide what they're talking about.'

'But if I were meeting someone I didn't know I'd take a friend to watch over me,' Peiperová insisted.

'Maybe she didn't have a friend. Or maybe it was a condition that she didn't.'

'How is he to know?'

'They meet somewhere where he can be sure he isn't seen. Somewhere very open where he can see if anyone is watching.'

'Such as?'

'A park. The zoo. That kind of place.'

Peiperová nodded. 'I can see that. But you'd think a sensible woman would at least tell a friend or arrange to telephone her afterwards.'

'Did Adalheid have a car?' Jerneková asked.

'Yes. It's parked outside her apartment.'

'But there's no sign that she was killed there or that she invited whoever it was to come back.'

'He must have known where it was. Remember he sent her a letter.'

'But did he send it there, or did he send it to her work? Why would she put it in her desk unless she had just received it?'

'What are you getting at?' Peiperová asked.

'He doesn't know where she lives but he knows where she works, so he sent the letter there. She suggested a meeting place. Perhaps she went there by public transport, or maybe it's within walking distance of her apartment.'

Peiperová pushed her chair back and drained her cup. 'Come on — work to do. You ring Barbora and see if she was out of town or uncontactable for any reason around the time Adalheid was killed. I'm going to look at the map to see her nearest metro stop. If we're very lucky there may be video footage and we may be able to get some idea where she was going.'

'She may have taken a tram.'

'She might, but we'll cross that bridge after we've looked into the metro option.'

Slonský was hung up on another aspect of the enquiry. Using the principle that his brain worked best when challenged by an intelligent interlocutor, and that the optimum conditions for cogitation were furnished in places where beer was readily available, he had nipped out for a small lunchtime lubrication. Valentin was eating what he persisted in calling breakfast, despite the hour, when Slonský caught up with him.

'Something bad happens to you, and you wait nearly forty years to take revenge. Why would you do that?' he asked.

'You're a Slovak?' suggested Valentin. 'They're not the quickest thinkers in the world.'

'Are you going to make a sensible suggestion or shall I give up now?'

'Well,' Valentin pondered, wiping his beard with his napkin, 'presumably when it happened the murderer was very young.'

'Yes, but he's had forty years to grow up, give or take. If he'd done it when he was in his twenties I could understand it.'

'Ah, but if you're talking about the case I think you're talking about, for the first twenty years or so Rezek was still high up in the StB and untouchable.'

'But his daughter never was,' Slonský pointed out. 'It sounds as if a sufficiently resourceful killer could have got to her at almost any time in her adult life. Of course, he'd have to flee the country afterwards, because Rezek's fury would be awful to behold.'

'But that's true now. Rezek isn't going to shrug his shoulders and forget this.'

'No, you're right, if I judge him correctly he's busy planning how he gets his revenge and he's decided for himself who the perpetrator must be. He's one step ahead of us because he has a name. We know whoever it is wrote to Adalheid Rezeková saying he had information on her husband's death, but he didn't sign the letter.'

Valentin took a gulp from his beer and noticed Slonský inspecting it closely. 'Today's one of my beer days,' he explained.

'Then this is a good day to ask your help. The little grey cells will be going flat out given the right fuel.'

'Maybe the killer has only just found out Rezek was behind his father's death?' Valentin suggested.

'It didn't take us long to tumble to that, and we had less information to start with.'

'Then maybe the thing that has held the killer back is that he only just found out where the bodies were buried?'

'You know,' said Slonský, 'for a journalist you can be surprisingly intelligent on occasions. There would be no point in doing anything to Rezek if that meant that the secret site of the burial was lost with him, because the collection of the remains was so important to him. It's not just about revenge — it's about reclamation and revenge.'

'He has to close two chapters here — not just one.'

'The bit that troubles me is that in this case the criminals are one step ahead of the police. Rezek knows who killed his daughter but he isn't telling us because he wants to deal with it himself. And whoever that is, killing Adalheid was only the first half of the job; the second part has to involve getting Rezek too, because until he does he isn't safe.'

'Not to mention that the real revenge will come when he has Rezek on his knees and pulls the trigger.'

Slonský looked closely at Valentin. 'You've got altogether too vivid an imagination for my liking. Are you sure you've got nothing to do with this?'

'As you may remember, my father only passed on fifteen years ago.'

'He was a good sort, your dad was.'

'He wouldn't have shot anyone. Not with his marksmanship.'

Chapter 12

Jerneková looked appallingly smug. 'Got it in one. Barbora was at a conference on the Wednesday. Eva Čechová thought it might be a romantic meeting, because she isn't a proper friend; she's a work colleague, whereas Barbora is both.'

'If we discount the dinner arrangement and assume it's just a meeting, perhaps that's why she blocked out the Thursday morning?' Peiperová suggested. 'It wasn't a hangover after a Wednesday dinner; it was a business meeting on the Thursday.'

'But she hadn't eaten for some time when she died. Is it likely that she'd missed breakfast?'

'Some women do.'

Jerneková shook her head. 'I don't know how they can. If I don't get something in the morning I'm likely to be snappy as hell.'

'You don't say.'

'You've got to admit I'm better than I was.'

'Ye-es,' Peiperová agreed in a half-hearted sort of way.

'This job has been great for me. Somewhere warm and dry to sleep and a bit of money in my pocket — that's all I ever wanted. I'll always be grateful to the Captain for making it happen.'

'I owe him a lot too. He brought me to Prague from Kladno. If it wasn't for him I'd never have met Jan, and we certainly couldn't have developed a relationship.'

'Maybe Jan should have him as his best man?'

Peiperová bit her lip. 'I don't know who he's having. Whenever I raise the topic he changes the subject. I just hope he's got someone.'

'Talking of changing the subject, did you get anywhere with the metro station?'

'The nearest station to her home was at Hloubětín. The shortest walking route to it takes her past a gun shop and a pharmacy, and they both have security cameras showing the street outside. Let's go and see if we can view the footage for Wednesday and Thursday.'

Slonský had given Navrátil a couple of hours off to go to a meeting about the apartment he and Peiperová had set their hearts on, so Krob and Slonský were going through some recent crime reports when the telephone rang.

'Have you got a minute?' Mucha asked.

'Should I make some time for you?' Slonský replied.

'I think you should. I can't come up — it's busy down here.'

'That's the trouble with criminals today — no consideration for the hard-worked desk sergeant.'

'It's serious, Josef.'

The fact that Mucha had used his first name was not lost on Slonský. It was a very rare occurrence, and the tone of voice betrayed some concern. Curiosity itself would have spurred Slonský to get himself downstairs as quickly as possible.

Mucha had a printout in front of him. 'I thought you should see this. We've had a report of a disturbance at a block of flats near Hůrka. A car was despatched. It sounds as if someone had their front door kicked in by an armed man. But read the description of the man.'

Slonský could read at speed when he wanted to, and it took him seconds to read the sheet. 'It's Rezek.'

'That's what I thought.'

'Good work, old friend. Do me a favour and tell Krob to get his rear end down here while I organise a car to take us out there.'

'Will do.'

Slonský turned to run off but was interrupted by a shout from Mucha, 'Josef! For once in your life, check your gun is loaded before you go.'

Krob was driving while Slonský read the main points of the report aloud.

'Call came in at 13:58 from a neighbour. Nobody seems to have heard Rezek arrive, but he knocked on the door. Our caller heard some shouting — something along the lines of "I know you're in there".'

'Why would he expect a man to be at home at that time of day?' Krob asked.

'Good point but I don't know,' Slonský replied. 'Anyway, after the shouting there was some more banging on the door, then he must have kicked the door in. The neighbour thought it was best not to look out at that precise moment, but she says she heard the visitor leaving about five minutes later, looked out of her window and saw a stocky elderly man with a stiff brush of grey hair striding to a car. She couldn't read the number at that distance but she says the car was dark blue.'

Krob parked the car and the two detectives ran into the block of flats. There was a uniformed officer standing guard outside a flat on the third floor which was missing its front door, or, more accurately, about two-thirds of its front door. They showed their badges and stepped carefully through the wreckage.

'No scenes of crime technician here yet?' demanded Slonský.

'Not yet, sir,' replied the uniformed officer.

'Be a good lad and use that radio of yours to pass on a message from me to the lab. Tell them I want someone here at the double. This break-in is connected to a murder enquiry so it gets bumped up the queue. Understood?'

'Yes, sir.'

Krob had peeked into each of the rooms. 'Our bird has flown, sir.'

'So it seems. Either that, or he's taking minimalist living to a new level. But if this is the flat of our murderer we've got two problems, Krob. It's hard to see how he could lower Adalheid's body from his window, and the little freezer in the kitchen wouldn't hold her handbag, let alone her corpse.'

'Rezek isn't a reckless or stupid man, sir. He must have some evidence telling him that this is the man he's looking for.'

Slonský looked around him. The furniture remained but all the personal items were gone. 'There's a thin layer of dust that suggests that nobody has been here for some time,' he said.

'Maybe he just doesn't like housework,' Krob replied.

'Any mail?'

'I'll see if I can check the pigeonholes by the front door, sir.'

There was a bundle of keys on the kitchen counter, and Krob slipped them in his pocket as he left in the hope that one of them opened the mailbox. Slonský continued to look around the flat and paused for a moment in the main room. Under a small glass table he found a ripped triangle of white paper. It was less than two centimetres long and perhaps a centimetre at its widest point, but Slonský carefully lifted it off the rug with the blade of a knife and dropped it into an evidence envelope from his coat pocket.

Pausing by the door he looked back into the room. Something seemed odd, but for a moment he could not think what it was, then it came to him. Returning to the bedroom he confirmed his finding and smiled to himself.

Krob appeared in the doorway with a collection of mail. 'Most of it is junk, but there are a few letters addressed to a František Kašpar, sir. Do you think he's our man?'

'I'm sure of it, Krob.'

'Why, sir?'

Slonský produced his evidence envelope. 'Exhibit one, lad. A small triangle of white paper with a shiny edge on one side. What does that suggest to you?'

'The flap of an envelope, sir.'

'That's a coincidence, because that's what I thought too. The flat had been cleaned meticulously but this fragment was on the rug, so I conclude that it wasn't there when the cleaning took place. Rezek opened an envelope and this little piece fell off.'

'Why would he open an envelope, sir?'

'Presumably because it was addressed to him, Krob. It can't be ordinary mail, because you've just collected that. I'm prepared to bet that Mr Kašpar knew that Rezek would work out who had killed his daughter and would eventually turn up at this flat wanting vengeance. And when he got here he found an envelope containing a letter addressed to him, and damn all else in the flat.'

'What was in it, sir?'

'I don't know because I haven't read it. Some taunting, perhaps, a confession, a threat, an invitation to a meeting — who knows? It wouldn't even surprise me if Kašpar had previously sent Rezek a note of his address.'

'Why would he do that?'

'Because it was taking Rezek too long to find him. I'm certain that Rezek knew who had killed his daughter from the moment Navrátil took him to the grave. It's taken him quite a while to turn up here, but I'm sure he's been trying to find out where Kašpar lives. Besides, think how much more Rezek must have been annoyed to be sent a letter telling him where to come and then finding Kašpar wasn't here. All he got for his trouble was another letter telling him to go somewhere else. His blood pressure must be through the roof by now, don't you think? Kašpar is piling on the agony.'

'Maybe that's why Rezek expected Kašpar to be at home. He'd said he would be.'

'It could be so, but if so Rezek would have been expecting Kašpar to be lying in wait on the other side of that door, and it would have been incredibly foolhardy to barge his way in. Isn't it more likely that Kašpar suggested an appointment and Rezek deliberately turned up early when he hoped Kašpar wouldn't be in? He shouted in the expectation that there would be no answer, but just in case he kicked the door in with his gun drawn. Look at the door, lad. It wouldn't take more than one or two kicks to get through it. I could do it with my slippers on. Anyway, there's more. Come with me.' Slonský led the way to the lounge and halted just inside the door. 'What do you notice, Krob?'

Krob looked around slowly. There were some fixed bookshelves on the wall, and a low cabinet on which a television set had once stood. In the centre of the floor was the glass table with steel legs, and two armchairs and a small sofa covered in a mix of burgundy and tawny stripes. Under the table was a sage green rug, and there was a standard lamp behind one of the chairs. Krob walked slowly round the room and paused by the window.

'The rug doesn't match.'

Slonský's face lit up. The boy was justifying the faith Slonský had shown in him.

'Quite right, lad. I'm no interior designer, but that just doesn't go. And, as I suspect you spotted, the floor by the window is a little paler, suggesting that the rug that was originally here was a bit larger than this one. If you take a squint in the bedroom you'll see there's no rug, although you're more likely to be padding around barefooted in a bedroom than a lounge, so if you've got one in the lounge, you'd certainly have one in the bedroom. I suspect this green rug would match the curtains in the bedroom better than it does here. So that causes me to ask myself where the rug from this room has got to, and what do I answer myself?'

'It was used to wrap the body.'

'Bingo! I hate to do this to you, lad, but we're going to have to reinstate the surveillance of Rezek's house. He's going to be going after Kašpar, and our best hope of catching Kašpar is to follow Rezek.'

'Sir, couldn't we just arrest Rezek for breaking in here? Then Kašpar couldn't carry out his attack because Rezek would be safe in a cell.'

Slonský shook his head. 'Why the hell would I want to keep Rezek safe, Krob? The man's a murderer. He deserves what's coming to him. If I frighten Kašpar off I'll have to find him myself and there's a chance Adalheid Rezeková, the innocent party in all this, will go unavenged. This way we can pinch the pair of them.'

'It's risky, sir.'

'Life is risky, lad. I should know. I've been eating in the police canteen for half of mine.'

Chapter 13

During the investigation Slonský had left Lieutenant Dvorník and Officer Hauzer to get on with their usual work rather than absorb all the available resources on a single case, but now that he needed to keep Rezek under surveillance it was time to brief Dvorník and Hauzer and put them to work.

Relationships between Slonský and Dvorník were surprisingly good, given Slonský's belief that Dvorník was a homicidal lunatic who had joined the police in order to provide an outlet for his gun mania. Dvorník belonged to a gun club and spent many hours at the police shooting range, and it had to be admitted that he was a good enough shot to be a sniper. He hunted regularly and had considerable confidence in his own ability, on one occasion shooting a suspect in the arm which was holding a knife to the suspect's wife's throat, an operation made even more hazardous by Slonský's belated realisation that he was standing in the line of fire and it was only the fact that the bullet lodged in the wife's shoulder that stopped Slonský suffering a nasty accident. This enraged Slonský so much that he stepped over the injured couple to remonstrate personally with Dvorník, temporarily overlooking the need to restrain the suspect whom Navrátil was attempting to disarm.

Even Slonský had realised that Dvorník had an issue with some aspects of modern policing. While he had no evidence that Dvorník had ever overstepped the mark with a witness, he had heard the lieutenant comment approvingly on threats made to them if they were not telling the truth, and now that Slonský was a captain he would have to take notice of them if they happened again; even if, as on previous occasions, Dvorník had been approving of something Slonský had threatened to do.

'It's really boring work watching a house,' commented Dvorník. 'Four hours is as long as most of us can concentrate for. That means six shifts. How about we get a couple of uniform guys to drive past a couple of times during the night and then divide the day into four four-hour shifts?'

'Sounds good to me,' Slonský replied. 'I can't see him being keen to leave his wife in the house on her own at night. If we have you, Hauzer, the two lads and the two lasses that means everyone gets a day off in three. I can't see it running on for long. In fact, I'd be surprised if Rezek isn't already planning his move.'

'There's no danger he'll get someone else to do it for him?' Dvorník asked.

'I don't think so. It's too personal. He'll want to see the whites of Kašpar's eyes as he puts a bullet in his forehead.'

'Do we have confirmation that the original body could be a Kašpar?'

'Novák is trying to get dental records for the other two bodies and I've asked him to add Kašpar to his search. Mucha is looking through our records for anything that might back up the identification.'

'If we find Rezek and it turns nasty, what are the rules of engagement?'

'He's a suspect, not yet convicted, so we only use force if he uses force on us.'

'So if he draws a gun, we can do so too?' Dvorník confirmed.

'I suppose.'

'Well, you never want to be the one who draws second, so I may just keep mine in my hand if I spot him.'

'Good plan,' Slonský agreed.

Dr Novák was not one to allow excitement to overrule his self-control, but when he telephoned he was very close to it.

'I've got hold of Toms' dental records, and he's a very close match to corpse three.'

'What does "a very close match" mean?' Slonský demanded.

'It means it matches very closely.'

'Yes, I got that much, but is it definitely him or not?'

'Slonský, there are over ten million people in the Czech Republic, and only so many ways a set of thirty-two teeth can be configured. By the law of large numbers alone, there must be a few people who would more or less match.'

'Then why do we use teeth to identify people?'

Slonský could hear Novák sighing.

'Forensic odontologists will —'

'Who?' Slonský asked.

'People who know about dead people's teeth.'

'Oh.'

'Forensic odontologists tell us that no two people have identical mouths. That is true. Given x-rays of teeth, we can identify people very well and with a high degree of certainty. The problem comes when we have a description but no actual pictures. The corpse has fillings where the chart says to expect fillings, and the most obvious feature is the loss of adjacent teeth either side of an old mandibular fracture...'

'Come again?'

'For heaven's sake, Slonský, somebody put their elbow into Toms' face while he was playing basketball. It's documented in his notes and those teeth are gone from the corpse, plus he has a healed break in the upper jaw.'

Why didn't you say that in the first place? thought Slonský.

'Bartek is another matter,' Novák continued. 'We haven't yet traced his dental records, but we did find his national service medical records, and corpse two is exactly the height that his records say he ought to be. I've asked for a facial reconstruction for each skull, but that takes time. All in all, I think you can take it that we've identified those two additional bodies.'

'What about the first corpse?'

'Slonský, I am a gifted pathologist but even I can't do much in the absence of a body.'

'I thought you had a fingertip or something?'

'Yes, and from it we have extracted some DNA. If you catch this Kašpar character, I should be able to take DNA from him and prove the relationship. But in the absence of any other known blood relatives in the first degree, I can't do much more.'

Slonský thanked Novák and was about to put the phone down when Novák spoke again.

'Wait, there's more! You know I said that Adalheid Rezeková's body had been in a freezer?'

'Yes, because you found ice on her.'

'Well, I was wrong. Or, at least, not entirely right.'

'Is there a difference?'

'Yes, of course there is,' Novák told him. 'Wrong means wrong as in not right. Not entirely right means partly wrong but also, ergo, partly right. The tissue samples show no biochemical signs that she was fully frozen. She was certainly kept in a very cold place, but not necessarily frozen. A walk-in refrigerator such as butchers use would be good enough.'

'But you still think she was wrapped in a rug?'

'We've got fibres to prove it.'

'I was in Kašpar's apartment. His furniture would have matched a red rug, but it's not there.'

'I'm not surprised. It would be forensically very useful. Fibres transfer from the rug to the body, but material will also pass the other way. If he had any sense he'd throw the rug away.'

'It'd be a large thing to dispose of. Maybe we'll have to scour the refuse dumps for it.'

'You could try. Personally, I'd take it to a cleaner.'

'To a cleaner? Why?'

'Because having it cleaned will destroy quite a lot of the forensic evidence, and if I give a false name and don't go back for it that gives somebody else the headache of getting rid of it.'

Slonský thanked Novák once more. As he returned the telephone to its cradle he reflected, not for the first time, that a pathologist who turned to homicide would be a very difficult adversary to nail. Except that Novák probably wouldn't be able to resist ringing the detective to tell him how clever he had been.

Peiperová's hunch had also paid dividends. Inspecting the video footage from Hloubětín produced a clear identification of Adalheid walking towards the metro station at 09:17 on a Thursday morning, presumably the day that she had been killed. She appeared to be wearing the clothes in which she had been buried. Following the image trail as far as she could, Peiperová could find Adalheid on the platform at Hloubětín, boarding a metro train on line B and alighting at Hůrka. She left the station there and no further pictures could be traced.

However, the video posed some interesting questions. Adalheid was carrying a handbag. At Hůrka she opened it, withdrew a folded piece of paper, and seemed to be looking for landmarks as if following directions. Where were the handbag and that piece of paper now?

Peiperová printed out a screen capture showing the handbag in as much detail as possible and made a second copy for Jerneková.

'Come on,' she said. 'The handbag wasn't with the body, it wasn't in his flat and he wouldn't want it to be found anywhere connected with him. It must be somewhere, though. So where would you get rid of a handbag you didn't want?'

'I don't know,' said Jerneková. 'I haven't had a handbag for years. If I didn't put it in the trash, I suppose I'd give it to a mate.'

'You and I could do that,' Peiperová replied, 'but it's not so simple for a man. Where could he get rid of a handbag?'

'It'll have to be the trash, then.'

'He can hardly take it to a recycling yard, and if he put it in his own bin we might have found it there. Besides, I think the waste management teams pick out handbags in case they've been stolen. We get descriptions of them from time to time.'

Jerneková twirled her hair around her index finger, which was the acknowledged sign that she was thinking hard. 'If we want to know what a man would do, why don't we ask a man?' she decided at length.

Peiperová shrugged her shoulders. 'Why not?' She tapped Navrátil's number into her mobile phone and waited for it to connect. 'Lucie is with me and you're on the speaker,' she commented, just in case Navrátil had it in mind to say something inappropriate. It had never happened before, but there is always a first time.

'Hello, Lucie,' said Navrátil.

'Ciao, Jan,' came the reply.

'Jan,' Peiperová continued, 'suppose you had a handbag and you wanted to dispose of it so that it wouldn't be traced back to you. How would you do it?'

'This is about Kašpar, isn't it?'

'Yes. I'm arguing that if he puts it in his trash it may be picked out as potentially stolen and reported to us.'

'He could heave it into the river. Or just leave it under a bush.'

'I suppose so. But there's always the risk that it will be found and traced back to him somehow.'

'Only if there's an appointment letter in there.'

Peiperová felt rather crestfallen. She had assumed that anyone who picked it up would do what she would do; report it to the nearest police station. But maybe a woman who found a handbag would just start using it.

'There's one other thing I can think of,' Navrátil broke in on her thoughts. 'He could leave it outside a charity shop.'

'That would do it,' agreed Jerneková. 'The best way of knowing it won't come back is to know that some other woman is using it.'

Hauzer was reporting, once again, that nothing was happening.

'You don't have to keep telling me that,' Slonský explained. 'If I know you'll tell me if Rezek is doing something, I'll deduce that when you don't say it it's because nothing is happening.'

'I'm not complaining, sir,' Hauzer said, 'but it's not the most exciting job I've ever done.'

'You've been watching too many detective shows on television, haven't you? The thing is that real police work is mostly tedious and boring, punctuated by the occasional burst of excitement when somebody shoots at us. This is the norm, lad. Long hours of sitting in cars watching paint dry. Whole afternoons typing a statement. Days of comparing notes to see where there's a difference. You'd better get used to it.'

Hauzer shifted in his seat because he believed that he might be losing the feeling in his rear end. 'Yes, sir,' he said.

'Lieutenant Dvorník will relieve you at 18:00. Don't bother coming back here. Just go home, Hauzer.'

'Yes, sir. Thank you, sir.'

'Don't thank me, thank Rezek. The moment he moves nobody gets any time off until we've nailed him.'

Physiologists tell us that adrenaline produces a series of changes in the body such that we do not feel the need to eat while under its influence. This makes evolutionary sense because stopping for a snack when you are running away from a lion may not be your best survival strategy. Slonský, on the other hand, often felt the need for a nibble of something when the chase was afoot, and preferred to fortify himself for potential future activity by keeping his blood sugar stores replenished at all times.

Thus it was that the realisation that Rezek might move at any time, including, horror of horrors, mealtimes prompted Slonský to slip down to the canteen to see if there was anything edible on the menu.

He read the chalked items from the menu board.

'What's Italian salad?' he asked.

'Sliced tomatoes and cheese,' Dumpy Anna explained.

'Then what's Greek salad?'

'Italian salad with a few olives chucked in.'

'Vegan quiche? How long have you been inflicting that on us?'

'Veganism is growing. There are several in this building.'

'Name the perverts.'

'I can't breach confidentiality like that!'

'You're not a priest or a doctor, Anna.'

'Well, there's Colonel Mach for a start.'

'I expect if you're the police service's head of dog handling you don't want to go near the cages smelling of meat. Who else?'

'Are you going to buy anything or are you practising for a new job as a food critic?'

'What have you got under the counter?'

'I could rustle you up a thick slice of smoked ham with some mustard.'

'You are a princess amongst women. I've always said so.'

Anna deftly sliced a roll open, laid the ham inside and flicked a spoonful of mustard over the top. She wrapped the sandwich in a paper napkin and told Slonský the price.

'How much? Don't I get the whole pig for that?'

'No, but I'm assuming you'll want your usual coffee to wash it down. I don't set the prices.'

'Yes, you do.'

'Alright, so I do. But I have guidelines and targets.'

Slonský fished out a couple of banknotes. 'Jesus Maria! I could have bought a vegan quiche for that. And it would probably have contained a whole vegan.'

He took his tray to a table and began eating his expensive sandwich. Glancing up, he saw Sergeant Mucha striding into the canteen in his overcoat. He dropped his cap on the table, unbuttoned his coat and sat down opposite Slonský.

'I thought I might find you here,' Mucha said.

'Not at these prices you won't. I'll take my business elsewhere.'

'You'll pay more, you tightwad. Now, shut up and listen, because I don't want my afternoon to have been wasted.' He reached across and tore a chunk off Slonský's sandwich before popping it in his mouth.

'Oi! You owe me twenty crowns for that mouthful.'

'I didn't have time for lunch, being on urgent police business on behalf of one Captain Slonský.'

Suitably chastened, Slonský gestured to Dumpy Anna to bring something for Mucha.

'This is the story of Tomáš Kašpar, father of František Kašpar. Are you sitting comfortably?' Mucha asked.

'Yes, but can't I just read it?'

'I wasn't allowed to bring the files away so I had to scribble some notes. You'll never decipher them.'

'That's true enough. I can barely read your writing at the best of times.'

Dumpy Anna placed a coffee and another smoked ham roll in front of Mucha.

'Nice to see you, Sergeant,' she said. 'If you want better company you could sit at the table over by the waste bin.'

Slonský held more money out and she tucked it in her apron pocket.

'I'll bring you your change,' she said.

'Don't bother,' said Slonský. 'I dare say it'll pay for your shoe leather walking over here.' He reached across the table and tore an end off Mucha's sandwich. 'We're quits now,' he announced as he tucked it into his mouth.

'It looks as if — what's wrong with you?'

'Holy God! What's in that sandwich?' Slonský spluttered.

'I like plenty of mustard. Proper mustard, not that tame stuff you get on the street stalls. Dumpy Anna knows that. Anyway, are you going to listen?'

'I'll have to. I can barely speak.'

'Stop being a drama queen. Tomáš Kašpar was born in 1935. Went to the University of Economics and earned a full set of degrees — bachelor's, master's and a doctorate. He specialised in something called dynamic resource allocation.'

'I haven't got a clue what that is and I bet you haven't either.'

'I wouldn't, but Klinger does, so I went upstairs to see him before coming here.'

'You went all the way up to the Fraud Squad offices? There's devotion to duty for you. Did Klinger have you chemically sprayed before he let you in?'

'No,' conceded Mucha, 'but I spotted him rubbing my chair with his handkerchief when I left.'

Major Klinger headed the Fraud Squad, which was something of a hyperbolic description for Klinger and his single remaining member of staff. Undoubtedly intelligent, rigidly methodical and obsessive about keeping his working environment clean, Klinger had never been seen in the canteen, but was rumoured to be the Czech police service's biggest consumer of coloured sticky notes.

'And what did Klinger tell you?' Slonský asked. 'Had he heard of Tomáš Kašpar?'

'No, but he says that's not surprising. Kašpar went to work as a civil servant for a while but he was still doing research part time. He became a dissident when he realised that the government's Five Year Plan worked by deciding what the country needed and then allocating materials and labour to make that happen, so in effect the whole economic system was locked in to the idea that things wouldn't change. Yet it was still subject to price fluctuations in the outside world that we couldn't control. Kašpar came to think that Communist economic theory was built on quicksand, and argued as much in a couple of memoranda.'

'You've proved the powers that be probably thought he was a grade A pain in the proverbial, but how does he get himself killed?'

'He was part of a delegation to West Germany in 1968, during the Prague Spring, and made some contacts there. He apparently impressed the West Germans, which immediately made the StB suspicious of him, and surveillance was stepped up considerably. When the West Germans had an election and changed their government, their policy towards the East changed.'

'See, that's what happens when you let ordinary people vote. They change things. That's why we gave it up for forty years.'

'Kašpar seems to have decided that the new West German policy was going to make life much easier for the Communist government here and he wrote to his West German friends to see if they could exert some pressure on their government to change the policy back. Of course, those letters never arrived. They're in his StB file. So it seems that he decided that he needed to go to West Germany. An agent provocateur planted amongst the dissidents reported on a meeting where this was decided.'

'I always think the "provocateur" bit suggests he was wearing women's underwear. Pray continue.'

'Those other two, Bartek and Toms, strongly supported Kašpar's plan, and they were deputed to get him out of the country and escort him if possible. Their first idea was to smuggle him on the team bus of Bartek's basketball team when they went to the West, but they got knocked out of some cup or other so that wasn't going to happen. They knew the border with West Germany was watched closely, so they hit on an alternative by doing the exact opposite.'

'You mean they'd sneak into Czechoslovakia?' Slonský asked.

'No, I mean instead of heading north-west they'd go south-east. They planned to get into Yugoslavia and then get to Greece or Italy, from where they could go on to West Germany. It might have worked if the sneak in their group hadn't told the StB all about it and they were picked up as soon as they set out.'

'So family and friends wouldn't worry about them for a few days because they weren't expecting to hear for a while.'

'They'd thought it could take three or four weeks to complete their journey and secrecy was important. They were taken for interrogation and in the end they went to the Red House so Rezek could use his skills on them.'

'And Kašpar and the others died under questioning?'

'Kašpar did,' Mucha confirmed. 'The others were executed, presumably by Rezek, to conceal the fact that the cell had been infiltrated and to stop news of what had happened leaking out. There's a note in the file from someone at the Ministry of the Interior rebuking Rezek for taking that action without checking with them first, but it goes on to say that since they would have approved they're not going to take it any further this time.'

'That's nice of them. It's good to know that summary execution of prisoners isn't necessarily a barrier to a long and successful career.'

'The file says that the bodies were disposed of before Kašpar could be examined by a doctor, but there's a letter from a pathologist in the file saying that the course of events suggests that Kašpar had an electrical defect in the heart, whatever one of those is, that messed up his heart rhythm. When Rezek gave him an electric shock it killed him.'

'Instead of just making him more talkative as usual. You know, up until now I thought that Rezek was a callous unfeeling bastard with a disregard for human life and dignity, but now I'm starting to dislike him.'

'You and me both,' Mucha agreed. 'So we know why František Kašpar wants to get his own back on Rezek, but we still don't know how he discovered all this given that he doesn't have access to the files.'

'Neither do we, strictly speaking.'

'Someone owes me a favour.'

'Yes,' Slonský conceded, 'but the point is that you knew where the files would be. Do you believe in coincidence?'

'Not really. But fortunately the wife does, so I can get away with coincidentally being on shift when her sister comes.'

'Your wife may, but I don't,' Slonský told him. 'Kašpar may have been brewing this for years but he wanted his father's body back and somebody told him where it was. And I doubt it was Rezek, so who else could have known?'

Chapter 14

Colonel Rajka summoned Slonský first thing in the morning, so Slonský dutifully turned up at Rajka's office only to be redirected to the police gymnasium where Rajka was keeping himself in trim.

As befitted a former Olympic wrestler, Rajka displayed grace, power and poise as he performed his exercises, demonstrating an ability to raise his chin above an elevated bar without much apparent effort in his arms. He may have been past forty years of age, but his physique was still impressive in his immaculate kit of maroon singlet, white shorts and white socks. On Slonský's rare visits to the gym he cut a less dashing figure in his kit (white singlet, shorts which may once have been navy blue and the first pair of socks that came to hand) and he was devoted to exercising with economy of effort.

'What do I need to know, Slonský?' demanded Rajka.

Since Rajka was doing some weird form of press-up that required only one arm to lift his body weight, Slonský was impressed that he was able to speak at all without wheezing.

Slonský ran through the evidence that had been collected.

'So we have enough to arrest this Kašpar character if we can find him,' Rajka remarked.

'Comfortably,' Slonský replied. 'I don't think he's especially worried about escaping. He just wants to buy time to finish the job.'

'You think he's going after Rezek?'

'I think he wanted Rezek to feel the pain of losing a close family member, which is why Adalheid was killed. There doesn't seem to be anyone else in Rezek's life about whom he cared much at all, except perhaps his second wife. But now that Rezek has had a bit of time to feel that grief, Kašpar will want to consummate his revenge. And that means putting a bullet through Rezek's skull, or some other inventive malice.'

'Are we giving Rezek any protection?'

'I have a rota of officers watching Rezek, but that was more from the point of view of stopping Rezek killing Kašpar before we found him. If Kašpar is going to nail Rezek, he has to lure him to a meeting. Following Rezek seems to me to be the best method we have of tracing where Kašpar has got to. He has to break cover to meet up with Rezek and when he does we need to be there.'

Rajka was casually tossing a dumbbell from one hand to the other as he thought. 'You're probably right,' he concluded. 'Just bear two things in mind. Rezek is no fool and he's trained to throw us off the scent. He's not going to be easy to follow. And if this all goes wrong we finish up with more bodies and a bit of explaining to do. Needless to say, I'll be delegating that explaining to you.'

Navrátil was hovering outside Slonský's office when the latter returned from the gymnasium.

'I wonder if I could have a word, sir,' said Navrátil.

'You regularly do,' said Slonský. 'Say your piece.'

'In private, sir,' Navrátil continued, and gestured towards Slonský's office door.

'You're not going to resign or anything daft like that?' Slonský asked.

'No, sir,' replied Navrátil, seemingly surprised that such a thought could have occurred to Slonský.

'That's all right, then,' said Slonský, and led the way into his room, indicating a chair in which Navrátil might have sat had he not noticed two folders, a coffee cup and a box bearing traces of pastries on the seat pad. 'Well, out with it, lad!'

Navrátil looked acutely uncomfortable. 'You know I'm getting married, sir?' he began.

'Good God, man, everybody in the place knows you're getting married. If it was meant to be a secret, I've got to say your fiancée hasn't done a great job of keeping it.'

'We hoped you'd be coming to the wedding, sir.'

'If invited, of course I will.'

The emphasis on "if" was not lost on Navrátil. 'The invitations are going out this week, sir. And of course you're getting one. May I ask if you want us to include Mrs Slonská too?'

That was a sore point. Slonský had been married to Věra for around two years when she ran off with a leather-jacketed poet, after which he had not seen her for another thirty, until she had reappeared about two years earlier. After a distinctly awkward spell they had started to spend a little time together, and it was clear that Věra hoped for a reconciliation. Slonský did not know what he hoped would come of it, but it had got as far as dinner on her birthday at which a man had recognised her and disclosed that her account of the missing thirty years was not entirely accurate, since he had been with her for about three of them. After that, they had not seen each other again, and although Věra had sent him a couple of notes he had decided not to reply.

'It's a kind thought, but I think I'll be unaccompanied, lad.'

'As you wish, sir. We just wanted to make the offer.'

'And it's appreciated, but if that's all...'

'It isn't all, sir. I was wondering if — that is to say — we had it in mind — what I mean is...'

'Spit it out, Navrátil, I won't bite.'

'I wondered if you would be my best man, sir.'

In forty years of adulthood Slonský had rarely been speechless, and he firmly believed that since he had seen everything there could be no surprises left, but he gulped air like a goldfish for a few moments.

'Don't you have friends of your own age?' he asked.

'Not really, sir. And we thought that since you brought us together…'

'Irina Gruberová brought you together,' Slonský answered, referring to the murder victim whose death he had been investigating when he took Navrátil to Kladno where they met Officer Peiperová, as she then was, with whom Navrátil was obviously and instantly smitten.

'You've known us as long as we've known each other, sir,' Navrátil continued, then, seeking to head off a possible objection, he quickly added, 'of course, there's no obligation to make a speech.'

Slonský stood up and extended his hand to be shaken. 'Young man, there are no circumstances in which I'm keeping quiet at this event.'

'Just to be clear,' Navrátil added, 'I wasn't planning on having a bachelor party.'

'What's a bachelor party?'

'It's what you see British tourists doing. The groom and his male friends go out drinking heavily and behaving stupidly.'

Slonský frowned. 'How is that different to a normal night out in Prague?' he asked.

The normal course of a police investigation does not follow a definite pattern, but they can be broadly divided into two types. In type A the culprit is immediately apparent, all the evidence points one way, there is an early confession and the police breathe a sigh of relief and add a tally mark to the crime statistics. In type B the evidence trail is partial, deduction gives way to guesswork and matters proceed at a glacial pace. If the crime is solved at all, it involves many hours of laborious comparison of statements; but once in a while, the enquiry takes a leap forward because something that Mucha would call intuition, Slonský would call experience and Valentin would call luck allows things to step up a gear.

Following his costly episode in the canteen Slonský had temporarily switched to lunching out, and he was skipping down the stairs to the front door debating which of two possible troughs he was going to dip his snout in when a question came to him. He had no idea why this had popped into his mind at that moment and not before since it was so obvious a question that he ought to have asked it much earlier, but better late than never.

Mucha was occupied in explaining to a tourist that the Prague City Police was an entirely separate organisation with its own stations, so Slonský waited until he was free so that he could ask his question.

'That folder you gave me,' he began.

'I've given you many folders. Which particular one?' Mucha asked.

'The one about Jiří Holub.'

'I remember. Go on.'

'Why did you get it?'

'Because you asked me to.'

'Ah — you misunderstand my question. It was exactly what I wanted, but how did you find it amongst so many other files?'

'I didn't. I asked the custodian to fetch it for me.'

'But why?'

'Because you asked me to find any examples of StB officers who had connections with the Red House.'

'We don't seem to be getting very far,' Slonský muttered. 'Why did you ask for Jiří Holub's file?'

'Ah, so that's what you're getting at. Because there was an item in the newspaper about him being released. I couldn't immediately remember his name but I remembered the article and I found it in that.'

Slonský slapped his hat on his head as if that might contain his rising blood pressure. 'Why didn't you tell me this before?' he asked.

'Because you didn't ask me,' Mucha replied in his most reasonable tone.

'So if you saw the story, it's possible that Kašpar saw it too.'

'Unless they only print one copy of each newspaper, I'd say it was entirely possible.'

'Therefore — follow me closely on this one — if Kašpar knew of Holub's existence, and eventually managed to track him down, which wouldn't be too hard because Holub is not that common a name, he may have heard through him about his father's death.'

'There are two problems with that,' Mucha replied. 'You told me that Holub wasn't working in the Red House at the right time. And didn't you also tell me that Holub denied outright that he had ever heard of a person being buried there?'

'He may have been lying,' Slonský responded. 'Criminals do, you know. I've complained about it but it does no good.'

Mucha clicked a few keys on his keyboard. 'Well, he's not lying about not having been there at the time. He hadn't joined the StB then.'

'But he may have lied about knowing anything.'

Mucha considered this proposition for a few moments. 'I've never met him, but you have. Did you think he was lying?'

Slonský shook his head. 'No, damn it, I didn't. But I suppose I could have been wrong.'

'Really?'

'Yes. It happened once in 1984, you know.'

'I find that hard to believe.'

'Does sarcasm come naturally to you, or have you had to work at it?'

'Compulsory training for a desk sergeant. You should know that.'

Navrátil and Peiperová had been granted a couple of hours off so they could sign the papers for their new flat. This had caused Navrátil some anxiety, because they were not yet married and therefore it was out of the question for them to share the flat before their wedding day. On the other hand, Peiperová thought it was foolish for them to pay rent on their existing lodgings when they had a perfectly good apartment they could be using. Accordingly, they had agreed a compromise. Peiperová would move in before the wedding so she could get the place ready for them, while Navrátil would remain in his existing flat until their big day.

Slonský had made it a condition of granting them the time off that he should be their first visitor, so, having carefully written down the address in his notebook, he promised to drop by after they had collected the keys, and then set out to interview Holub once more.

This time Holub was not as suspicious as he had been the first time. This may have been a mistake on his part, because he had just opened the door and turned his back on Slonský to return to his chair when he found himself grabbed by the scruff of the neck and pushed face first against the wall.

'You didn't tell me anyone else had been asking about deaths at the Red House,' Slonský growled.

'You didn't ask,' protested Holub.

'You know better than that. You knew what I was getting at and you could have saved me a lot of trouble by volunteering the information straight out.'

'What's to tell?' Holub protested. 'I told you I didn't know anything and that's what I told him too.'

'But you didn't mention it to me.'

'To be honest it slipped my mind. It was not long after I got out. He badgered me, and I told him to leave me alone because I knew nothing that could help him.'

'But you did help him, didn't you?' Slonský persisted.

'I put him on to Jelínek. I don't know whether that helped or not.'

'And how would he get in touch with Jelínek, because you told me you didn't know where he lived?'

'I don't. I've no idea how he found him.'

'But you know he did?'

'He came back to say he'd traced Jelínek,' Holub admitted. 'He gave me a few crowns and told me to forget we'd ever spoken.'

'You seem to have managed that quite well.'

'I'm not in a position to refuse a thousand crowns, right? Look, if you're going to take it out on me, just do it and get it over with.'

Slonský thought briefly, then relaxed his grip and allowed Holub to turn to face him. 'No, you're not worth it. And I'll take into account the difficult position you were in. But you should still have told me. Next time, if there is a next time, you squeal before you're hit, got it?'

Holub nodded sullenly.

'And you swear you have no idea how he found Jelínek?'

'He didn't say. No, wait, when I asked him how he found me he told me he worked for the city authorities so he had access to name and address records. Maybe that was it.'

Slonský felt nonplussed. After so long with no forward momentum the enquiry was running away from him. It had not occurred to him to check what Kašpar did for a living. Was it possible that this was the first sign that his brain was beginning to age?

No, he decided, it was due to the lack of suitable brain fuel.

'Come on,' he said to Holub. 'I need a beer. Fetch your coat.'

Jerneková's feet were aching, but she felt triumphant. At long last she had an achievement of her very own to crow about. The snag was that she had no idea where Slonský was and the two lieutenants were off collecting their flat keys, so the only person she could discuss it with was Krob.

She liked Krob. He was quiet, a decent family man, seemed to dote on his wife and was unfailingly polite. Admittedly, by the standards of many Czech men she had encountered he would have appeared polite by not being abusive, but there was something unflappable about Krob. He was more patient than she was, but then so were ninety-nine per cent of the population.

Krob was sitting at his desk writing a note when she tapped on the door and invited herself in.

'Got a moment?' she asked.

'Of course,' Krob replied. 'Just let me finish this sentence, if you don't mind.'

He did so and laid down his pen to indicate his readiness to listen.

'I've found Adalheid's handbag,' Jerneková told him. 'Well, not her handbag as such, because they've sold it, but the second-hand shop where it was left.'

'Well done! Any description of the person who left it?'

'No, nobody saw it being left. They have a box by the door where people can leave stuff and it was in there in a black plastic sack. The assistant remembered that it looked far too good to throw away.'

'Any contents?' Krob asked.

'Clean as a whistle. But it's just eight hundred metres from Kašpar's home.'

'That's interesting. Captain Slonský just rang me and asked me to find out what Kašpar did for a living.'

'And what was that, then?' Jerneková asked.

'He was a transport manager for the city council.'

'Which means?'

'He had access to the city's computer systems. He would also have been able to get the vehicles he wanted.'

'Like that little electric thing you were talking about him using to move the body?'

'Yes, but I've discovered something more interesting. The city own a lot of vehicles, but they also take some specialised ones on short-term hire, and Kašpar was authorised to hire these. And I think I know where Adalheid was kept from Thursday until the weekend, when he could dispose of her where he wanted.' Krob produced a faxed copy of a hire document.

'A refrigerated van?' Jerneková asked.

'The kind they use to transport meat and fish. He could keep her in there for as long as he needed. And he returned it on the Monday after she was buried.'

'Why didn't he use it to transport the body?'

'Perhaps he did. But I think the reason why he might not have done is that it has the hire company's name on the side in big orange letters. Maybe it was just too noticeable.'

Slonský did not wait to be invited in.

'I should have smelled a rat when you were able to trot out a story from nearly forty years ago without any hesitation,' he said. 'But then that was because you'd recently been reminded of it, wasn't it?'

Jelínek was doing his best to look like a grumpy old man, in which attempt he was succeeding rather well. 'It's not my job to do your work for you,' he grumbled.

'No, but you could have told us that someone had been round asking.'

'Must have slipped my mind.'

'Let me ask you another question, and if you have trouble recalling the answer I can give your head a sharp tap with my fist to dislodge the memories for you. Did you tell the young man which grave was his father's?'

'Not exactly.'

'How do you mean, "not exactly"?'

'I told you I didn't know the names, and I don't. This young fellow did, and when he told me I could remember which was which. But I'm an old man. I forget these things, and when he'd gone I forgot the names again, so I wasn't lying when I told you I didn't know.'

'But you must have guessed why Adalheid Rezeková ended up in that grave?'

Jelínek had the grace to look a little shamefaced. 'I guessed, of course. But he never said anything about her to me. It was Rezek he wanted.'

'Did he know the name Rezek or did you tell him?'

'He didn't know for sure. He'd been trying to look into his father's death for years, he said, but he didn't know for certain who killed him. I said I thought it was probably Rezek.'

'Probably? Only "probably"? So, for all you know, Adalheid Rezeková may have died for something her dad only "probably" did.'

'No, I knew he'd done it. I just didn't want to get involved. Those days are past now. All the public is interested in now is revenge.' Jelínek's eyes burned as he complained about the injustice of it. 'They go after us now, loyal servants of the State, but they don't get the kingpins, do they? The Rezeks of the world are allowed to retire to their nice villas and grow a few cabbages in peace. It's people like me, the ones who had to carry out the orders, we're the ones who get sacked and can't get another job, we're the ones who get banged up for our so-called past crimes, we're the ones who finish up living in this latrine of a flat with a one-bar fire for company. If Rezek was going to pay for what he'd done, damn good thing in my eyes. I'd hold the lad's coat while he filled Rezek with lead. If I had a gun I'd let him have a few myself, except I can't get a licence on account of being a convicted ex-StB man.' Jelínek crossed the room and dropped into his armchair. 'Going after his girl, that's different. I don't hold with that. But it wasn't mentioned.'

Slonský moved some papers to clear a space where he could sit. 'Let's get one thing straight. I served in those days too. I did things I didn't like because I was ordered to. I get that. Youngsters today say we could have refused to do them. We know better. But those days have gone, and by God if I have anything to do with it they aren't coming back. We have to be clean today. We have to do what we can to put right what we did wrong. Doing more wrong is not the way to go about that. I don't care how old Rezek is, if I can nail him for the murder of Tomáš Kašpar, he's going behind bars.'

'Yes,' said Jelínek, 'in a cushy open prison with proper heating, three meals a day, a library. Jesus Maria, he'll suffer! I've got half a mind to commit murder myself. I'd be a damn sight better off in jail. For a start I'd have people to talk to.'

'Do you think Rezek's going to enjoy his time in prison once his fellow inmates find out his past? Once they hear he was a high-ranking StB officer, how long do you think he'll last before he unaccountably sticks his head down a toilet till he drowns?' Slonský stood up, planted his hat on his head and made for the door. 'I'll see myself out,' he said.

Chapter 15

Slonský was impressed, and said so. He had never seen so much white in a building. The walls were white, the doors were white, the kitchen work surfaces were white. It was as if Navrátil had earned his promotion to angel early.

Peiperová was busily showing him the many and varied ways that the designers had found of concealing storage spaces in the kitchen, to the point where Slonský pressed hopefully on a wall half expecting a shelf to leap out at him.

'No, that actually is a wall, sir,' Navrátil told him.

Slonský amused himself for a while opening and closing the pedal bin with his foot, glancing at his watch as if timing the response. 'What a view you have from that window!' he cooed. 'Help me get my bearings here. What church is that?'

Navrátil and Peiperová pointed out several features of interest at which Slonský showed his enthusiasm with repeated exclamations, each a little louder than was appropriate in Navrátil's view.

When they turned round to face into the room they were surprised to see a small man with the facial expression of an antique ferret sitting on the sofa.

'Who are you?' Navrátil demanded.

'Let me introduce you,' Slonský intervened. 'This is Mr Fingers. He has a proper name but you don't need to know it. He is my wedding present to you.'

Navrátil and Peiperová goggled at each other while trying to frame an appropriate response.

'He's very nice, but I don't know where we'll keep him,' Navrátil finally croaked.

'No, you misunderstand me. It's his services that form the present, not the man himself, who, frankly, wouldn't go with the décor.'

'It's very … white, isn't it?' said Mr Fingers.

'As you will have noticed, Mr Fingers was able to enter your flat with the minimum of noise.'

'What is he — a burglar?' asked Peiperová.

'Reformed,' Mr Fingers protested.

'Now working as — what shall we say? — an independent security consultant,' Slonský explained.

'That's good. I like that,' said Mr Fingers. 'I must get some business cards made with that on.'

'Anyway,' Slonský continued, 'as a result of our lengthy professional relationship, I can vouch for the fact that a building that Mr Fingers cannot get into is secure indeed. And his job is to make your flat one of them. By the time he has finished here an emaciated fly won't be able to squeeze in.'

When he had created the rota for covertly watching Rezek's house, Slonský had forgotten that Jerneková did not drive; or, perhaps more accurately, the fact that she did not drive would mean that she did not have a car to hide in when conducting her observations. As a result, after she rang Krob to find out where he was observing from, he was more than a little surprised to find her climbing into his car.

'You haven't got a car?' Krob said.

'No point. No licence, have I?'

'But if I leave you the car I'll have to come back for it later. I don't want to be difficult but that's a bit of a problem.'

'I could just lock it up and bring the keys back to you.'

'You could, but then I'd have to make my own way out here by bus tomorrow night.'

Jerneková knitted her brow. 'How do you think I got here, then?'

'I don't know. I didn't give it any thought.'

'I had to make my own way by bus. At least Captain Slonský told me I didn't need to wear uniform for this assignment.'

'It would be a bit obvious to even an old man if a policewoman was sitting near his door.'

'Or a policeman. It's the uniform that's the giveaway, not the sex.'

'I suppose. Look, why don't I ring Captain Slonský and see what he suggests?'

Slonský arranged for a police car to meet Krob in some discreet corner, and undertook to send one to collect Jerneková at the end of her shift so that she could return the keys to Krob, who would be collected tomorrow evening to complete his next shift. He rang Sergeant Vyhnal on the reception desk to ask him to put it all into effect, and then relaxed again, confident that Vyhnal would make it all happen.

'I didn't realise there were policewomen who don't drive,' Valentin remarked.

'I think we have to say police people now,' Slonský retorted.

'Do we?'

'Hang on,' said Slonský. 'You don't drive either.'

'I never felt the need. There's nowhere to park and yobs pull your hubcaps off if you leave it in the street.'

'I wonder what our generation did for mindless vandalism before car ownership became widespread?'

Valentin considered a moment, taking a large gulp of beer to aid his recollection. 'You remember those big black and white photos of party leaders they used to hang all around town during Party Congresses and the like?'

'Of course I do.'

'Well, Honza Langer and I used to have competitions to see who could urinate furthest up them.'

'And did you excel at this urban sport?'

'No, Honza was much better than me. But I did once get First Secretary Novotný right on the hairline.'

'I'm impressed. Shame it wasn't the man rather than his poster.'

'I wonder what Honza's doing now?'

'I can't see him getting a job on the strength of that particular skill.'

'Firefighter?' suggested Valentin.

'I think the fire service prefers more reliable sources of water than Honza's bladder, but it's a thought.'

'May I say,' said Valentin, 'that for a man with four murders to solve you're remarkably relaxed this evening.'

'That's because I've solved the four murders. Kašpar killed Rezeková, and Rezek killed Kašpar senior, Bartek and Toms.'

'Then why don't you arrest Rezek?'

'Two reasons,' Slonský told him. 'First, those incompetents in the Prosecutor's office keep banging on about having this thing called "evidence", which is a little hard to procure thirty years after the killing. It's pretty unreasonable of them, in my view, but it seems to matter to them. Then there's the second problem, which is that if I put Rezek under lock and key I prevent Kašpar getting at him, and at the moment Rezek is the best bait I have for flushing Kašpar out.'

'Can't you find Kašpar some other way?' Valentin asked.

'We're doing all the usual things like tagging his credit cards and bank accounts, but he hasn't used them since the day when Rezek broke into his flat. We can't find the car that's registered to him.'

'So what do you think was in that envelope Rezek opened in Kašpar's flat?'

'I don't know exactly, but it probably contained a few taunts and insults, told him that Kašpar knew he'd killed his father and let Rezek know that Kašpar was going to kill him too.'

'So why isn't Rezek asking for protection?' Valentin persisted.

'He can't without showing us the letter that says he's a murderer. Besides which, it's not in Rezek's nature to ask for help sorting his problems out. I may not have met Rezek before, but I've met his type, and if I'm any judge his idea is to get Kašpar before Kašpar gets him.'

'Isn't that all the more reason to run him in to prevent bloodshed?'

'Why? If one of them bumps off the other it saves the country an expensive trial and the costs of keeping someone in clink. Win-win, I'd say.'

'So why hasn't Rezek done anything?'

'Because he doesn't know where Kašpar is,' Slonský said. 'But the fact that he isn't looking suggests to me that the mysterious letter may have contained an appointment. Rezek isn't searching because he knows where Kašpar will be at a certain time and date.'

'So couldn't he give that to you and you could pick Kašpar up with no danger to Rezek?'

'He could, but it's a coward's way out in his eyes. He'll want to deal with this once and for all. After all, suppose Kašpar escapes us. He's going to feel double-crossed. Rezek won't get another appointment, just a bullet in the head when his back is turned.'

'How long are you going to have to wait?'

'Not long, I think. Kašpar wrote the note and presumably told Rezek where to find it, but by then he'd cleared out of his flat and collected most of his savings. I think he's already gone to the rendezvous point to ensure that Rezek can't get there first and ambush him.'

'You think he's sleeping rough?'

'That depends where the rendezvous is, doesn't it? For all we know, he may have booked into a five-star hotel in an assumed name.'

'If that's the case, it's even more reason to prevent a shootout. Someone could get hurt.'

'Yes, and I'd rather that someone wasn't me,' Slonský told him, 'which is why I'm sitting here having a beer with you. Fancy another?'

Chapter 16

Sunday was officially a day off for Slonský, but since he had nothing better to do and he found sitting in his flat depressing, he did what he normally did on his days off and went to work. Much to Slonský's surprise, he was not the only person who worked on their day off. The light was on in the women's office, and when he investigated he discovered Jerneková was sitting at her desk engrossed in something on her monitor and surrounded by the remains of an eclectic meal.

'I'm sure that diet can't be good for you,' he said.

'Good afternoon, sir. I like pickles. What more can I say?'

'Most people have pickles with other things. Besides yoghurt, that is.'

Jerneková shrugged. 'I like pickles, and I like yoghurt. Can't get enough of the stuff. Why eat stuff you don't really like?'

'When you put it like that,' Slonský replied, 'I wonder why I've wasted so much of my life eating carrots. But what are you doing here?'

'I can't get a question out of my head, so I thought I'd better find an answer.'

'What's the question?'

'How did Kašpar find Adalheid Rezeková? Or even know that she existed?'

'Good question. And have you found an answer?'

'Sort of. She's in the phonebook, so he can get her address. And obviously a Rezeková is the daughter or wife of a Rezek. But it was the link with her father that I wanted to pin down. Killing her only makes sense if Kašpar knows she's the general's daughter. They don't have much to do with each other, so he's unlikely to have seen them together. Then I found this.' She clicked on her screen and it filled with a blurry image. 'If you search for Klement Rezek on the internet you don't find much but there is this guide to senior StB officers that someone put together around 1990. There's a photo and a potted biography which mentions that he has a son and a daughter. But of course the son doesn't use his father's surname, so he can't easily be found. That leaves the daughter.'

'And a father would be more upset about failing to protect a daughter than a son.'

'If you say so,' answered Jerneková, who seemed to be unconvinced, to judge by her sceptical tone.

'So it would be quite possible for Kašpar to know that Rezek has a daughter. And then he could use his access through the local council to find out where she lives.'

'I thought that, but it's not quite so easy as that. And I got the impression that the letter she hid had been delivered to her work, not her home, so I tried to find her through the addresses database, but the address for her is an old one. She must have moved flats and the database hasn't caught up.'

'And now you're going to tell me how clever you've been in working out how it was done?' Slonský asked.

'Not really. It was child's play. An internet search threw up a profile of her in a women's business magazine. Obviously it says where she works, and there aren't that many Adalheid Rezekovás around.'

Slonský scanned the article on the monitor. 'She looks a lot better alive than she does now,' he concluded. 'Good work, lass. That tidies up a loose end.'

'Thank you, sir. Have you been in your office yet? I left a note on your desk.'

'What does it say?'

She closed her eyes as if recreating the note in her head. 'It says that Colonel Rajka presents his compliments, and if you could find time in your busy diary to get your rear end into his office he would appreciate it. Words to that effect, anyway.'

'I'll make a point of seeing him some time tomorrow. If time permits.'

Navrátil had suggested that he and Peiperová go out for their evening meal, and a couple of hours later they were standing outside their new flat, with Peiperová feeling ready to retire for the night. There was only one problem — there appeared to be more locks on the door than he had keys for.

Navrátil used the key he had, and the door opened. On the floor he saw an envelope addressed to them both that had been taped to the wood, so he prised it free and opened it. It contained some keys and half a dozen pieces of plastic with bar codes on them.

'Have you won something?' Peiperová asked.

'No, it's Captain Slonský's wedding present. There's a list of which new key opens what. We've now got two locks on the front door, locks on each window, and an alarm system we set and unset using these little tags. There's also a spyhole in the door and a pressure pad under the mat outside that connects to this little light above the door to tell us if someone is standing there.'

'This must have cost Captain Slonský a fortune,' Peiperová remarked.

'Yes,' agreed Navrátil, 'but he probably doesn't know that yet.'

Slonský opened his wallet and found the requisite sum.

'You carry a lot of cash around,' said Mr Fingers. 'You want to be careful. There's a lot of crime in Prague these days.'

'Not while I'm around, there isn't. And it must have reduced since you went straight.'

'True. I miss the buzz, but to be honest housebreaking is a young man's game. I'm not up to clambering through skylights these days.'

'Just for the avoidance of doubt, none of the stuff you installed was nicked, was it?'

Mr Fingers paused in mid-slurp to look affronted. 'What do you take me for? I'm not into receiving stolen property.'

'No, but it would be a great joke at my expense to install stolen security equipment in the home of two police officers paid for by a third.'

'I've got the receipts if you want to check. Well, except for the pressure pad. I got that off a mate and I didn't ask him where he got it from.'

'Thanks for doing it so quickly. Are they pleased with it?'

'I don't know,' said Mr Fingers, donning his cap and pea jacket. 'We didn't exactly make an appointment with them. But I figured you wouldn't do me for breaking and entering to install extra security. Which was badly needed, by the way. A novice with a fine blade could have been in there within half a minute.'

'I thought as much. The trouble is a lot of housebreakers these days just take a sledgehammer to the front door, run in and grab what they can.'

'Yes, I know. That's why I put a "Beware of the rottweiler" sign next to their doorbell. See you around.'

Chapter 17

Monday morning dawned bright and sunny, which is more than could be said for the disposition of Colonel Rajka.

'Let's get this straight, Slonský. I give you a great deal of latitude to do your work in your way. I don't interfere. In exchange for that, I expect you to keep me up to date with developments. If you don't, I will have to sit on your shoulder all the time, and neither of us would like that.'

'No, sir,' agreed Slonský.

'Incidentally, I see congratulations are in order.'

'Sir?'

'According to your personnel folder, last Friday you completed five full years since your last disciplinary hearing.'

'Really? I don't think I've done a five-stretch before.'

'Take that Švejk expression off your face. I've managed nineteen years without one. Let's see if we can get you through to retirement without another.'

Slonský shuddered. He reacted to the R-word rather like cats respond to seeing a bath being run for them. 'I don't know if I can manage to stretch it to ten years, sir,' he said hopefully.

Rajka clicked his mouse a few times. 'Let's see when your retirement date is. Born 1949, I see. That gives you about four and a half more years.'

Slonský could hardly suppress his joy. His little ruse had added two years to his working life by deducting two from his real life.

'That smirk is back again, Slonský.'

'Sorry, sir. Natural ebullience at the thought of four and a half years of continued service, sir.'

'I'm delighted you feel that way. Now, back to the point. I approved your plan not to arrest Rezek because I didn't like the idea of the tabloids leading with headlines about "Grieving father of murder victim arrested" when we don't have much evidence other than Kašpar's clear belief that Rezek was responsible.'

'I suppose Kašpar may have some evidence, once we manage to find him.'

'Slonský, call me old-fashioned but I'm not exactly keen on the idea of the police relying on murder suspects to provide evidence on other murder suspects. I have this quaint idea that we should do most of the evidence gathering ourselves.'

'Very commendable of you, sir. For what it's worth, I agree.'

They were interrupted by a sharp knock at the door. Rajka barked a command to enter, and Navrátil leaned in. It did not look as if he planned to stay long.

'Sorry to interrupt, sir, but Hauzer has been in contact. General Rezek has loaded up his car and is on the move.'

'Is Hauzer sure he isn't going to the supermarket?' asked Slonský.

'Not unless he needs an ammunition clip and a camouflage jacket to go shopping, sir.'

'Right. Get Hauzer to follow him. Who's in the office?'

'Just Krob and me, sir. Lieutenant Dvorník is in his office, and Peiperová and Jerneková are going back to Ms Rezeková's office.'

'Then you and Krob take one car and follow Hauzer, and divert the women to follow you as soon as they can. I'll come along with Dvorník. And tell everyone that he's armed.'

'Yes, sir.'

Slonský turned to look at Rajka.

'There are enough of you there not to need me in the way,' Rajka said, 'so I'll stay here. If you need backup, call me and I'll arrange it.'

'Thank you, sir.'

Slonský made for the door.

'And Slonský, please remember, he may be an old man, but he's not a man to trifle with. No unnecessary risks.'

Dvorník drove in the same way as he used guns, aiming the car in such a way as to terrify others. Since this tallied fairly well with Slonský's own method of driving, which also involved adding five kilometres per hour to the speed limit, Slonský settled back to enjoy the drive.

It soon became clear that he ought to have charged his mobile phone, because once he had called everyone a few times to check their progress he decided to save his battery for emergencies and use the radio system. This had the disadvantage that others might hear his messages, which was one reason why he rarely used it. The other main reason was that he had forgotten how and therefore blithely ignored the usual conventions for radio communications. On this occasion the easy thing was to leave it to Dvorník, who could, it seemed, drive a car entirely with his left hand and one knee while he worked the radio with his right hand. The exhibition reminded Slonský of an elephant he had once seen at a circus who could balance a football on an upraised knee, and he was tempted to offer Dvorník a banana to see if he could manage the rest of the act by feeding himself with his trunk.

'Hauzer says he's heading along highway 4 towards Příbram,' Dvorník announced.

'So I heard,' said Slonský. 'That won't be the final destination. It's too public.' He unfolded the map of the country. 'Could he be heading for Šumava National Park?'

Dvorník was sceptical. 'There are lots of pathways and rangers around. How could you set an appointment in advance and know there wouldn't be an audience?'

'If I'm right, and Kašpar has been there for a few days, he could have marked a path as closed, for example. Or maybe he's made the appointment for one of those huts and he'll leave directions there for Rezek to pick up.'

Slonský knew that Navrátil and Krob were a few kilometres ahead of them, whilst the women were an unknown distance behind. Peiperová would be driving, and she was competent at high speed.

'We've got to be careful we don't get ahead of him,' Slonský announced on the radio. 'We can go faster with our sirens on than he can, so take care not to scare him off. Hauzer, give everyone your registration number so we don't pass you.'

'I can't, sir,' came a plaintive voice. 'I don't know it. It's a pool car.'

'At least give us the colour and model, lad,' Slonský snapped.

'It's a silver Škoda Fabia, sir.'

'That'll narrow it down a bit,' muttered Slonský. 'There can't be more than a hundred thousand of them on the roads.'

'I'll wind down the passenger window, sir. That should help to identify me.'

'Good idea, Hauzer. Have you got electric windows, then?' Slonský asked enviously.

'No, sir. Just long arms. We're just coming to the outskirts of Příbram now so he's got to slow down a bit.'

Slonský returned to scrutiny of his map. It was around a hundred and eighty kilometres from Prague to the park, so if he was right about the destination they would be driving for around two and a half hours. He wished he had had a bigger breakfast; and maybe brought a sandwich or two and a flask of coffee.

Hauzer was doing a good job of tailing Rezek. It is not easy to follow a car through a suburban area where traffic lights are likely to change after the front car has passed and thus slow down the follower, but Hauzer had managed to retain visual contact until they were back in open country.

Dvorník pointed to his rear-view mirror. 'There appear to be two demented women in the car behind waving at us,' he said.

Slonský wound down the window and waved his arm in acknowledgement of their presence. 'Peiperová has done well to catch you,' he said. 'You don't hang about.'

They drove on, and Slonský's supposition about Rezek's destination appeared to be borne out as the old man ignored the turn to Plzeň and ploughed on towards Strakonice. Not long after they passed Strakonice Dvorník tucked in behind Navrátil's car so the three cars were driving in convoy.

'Once he's parked, we'd better hang back until Hauzer reports he's out of sight of the road,' Slonský said. 'Dvorník, are you any good at disabling cars? I want to make sure Rezek can't make a quick getaway.'

'I could shoot his tyres out,' Dvorník suggested.

'No loud noises. Just let one of them down.'

'Do we know his registration number?'

'Good point. It'll be a dark blue car with a silver Škoda Fabia parked nearby. Get on the radio to Mucha and see if he can find the registration number for us.'

A little under an hour later Hauzer announced that Rezek had turned off the road and parked near Borová Lada at the entrance to the national park.

'Follow on foot, lad. Don't take any chances.'

'No, sir. Shall I let one of his tyres down?'

'Good idea. I'm glad you thought of that.'

Hauzer watched Rezek leave his car and begin walking up a trail into the forest. He waited two or three minutes before climbing out of his own vehicle, letting some air out of Rezek's front nearside tyre, and following along the trail.

When the three cars arrived, Slonský directed them to park well away from Rezek's car so that he would not be suspicious of their presence.

Together the six detectives walked to a display board which showed the geography of the park.

'Unfortunately I daren't ring Hauzer in case Rezek hears the phone, but let's assume he's following the main path,' said Slonský.

There was a finger of flat land that cut into the forest leading south-west from the village. A path curved away to the right entering the forest after about three hundred metres and another path diverged from the main one to the left and entered the forest on that side.

'There are so many ways out of the forest but in the end he has to come back to his car, so if we cover those three we should be able to trap him. Peiperová and Jerneková, you take the right hand path, Navrátil and Krob, you go left, and Dvorník and I will proceed up the centre. Remember that these men are dangerous. I want them alive if at all possible. If you have to shoot, shoot to disable rather than kill, but if push comes to shove I'd rather see one of them dead than one of you. All clear?'

There were exclamations of assent and the pairs split up to do their work. Navrátil and Krob returned to the car to collect their weapons but Slonský and Dvorník walked straight on.

'Shame I didn't go home first,' said Dvorník. 'I've got the ideal rifle for this job there. It can take the eyebrows off a marmot at fifty metres.'

'Well, if we're threatened by an armed marmot I'll bear that in mind,' Slonský replied.

They had progressed to the end of the flat section and were climbing slowly into the forest when they came across Hauzer, who was lying face down in some bracken. Slonský rolled him over and was delighted to see that he was breathing and conscious, if groggy, though the side of his head displayed signs of a blow from someone behind him.

'It shows we're on the right track,' Slonský commented grimly.

'He obviously wasn't as discreet about his following as he thought,' Dvorník replied. 'He'll be okay, but his head's going to hurt. I'll call for an ambulance.'

'Okay,' said Slonský. 'I'll keep going for a while and you can catch me up.'

Slonský's shoes may have been adequate for an office job, but they were not the best option for a hike on a mountain trail in the forest, and he slipped a couple of times on loose material as he climbed steadily upwards. He tried telephoning the other pairs as he went but his declining battery, and poor phone signal in the forest, meant that he was not able to reach them.

This did not concern him too much, because he had learned to have confidence in his lieutenants.

On a Monday morning in spring there were not many people about and none at all in the area where Rezek had headed. The sky was blue, there was a bright sun, and if it had not been for the breeze Slonský would have found it quite enjoyable. That, and the absence of food — and the exercise. Together they were making it a fairly miserable experience for a rather portly (Slonský would have preferred "well-built") middle-aged man.

On top of everything else, the birds in the trees were keeping up a spirited conversation with each other, making it difficult for him to think. Objectively, a few woodland creatures cannot make as much noise as the population of Prague, but urban sounds did not seem to disconcert him so much. He had grown up with those and was perfectly capable of snoozing through a convoy of lorries rattling his windows, but the sound of a starling was enough to prevent him getting any more sleep. Glancing up at the trees he detected a wide variety of different birds, but that was as far as his ornithological knowledge would stretch. Asked to describe the wildlife, he would have been reduced to "Bird, type 1", "Bird, type 2" and so on. Had there been an owl around he might have done a little better.

He was just wondering whether any of the fungi he was passing were edible when he heard a loud noise. The birds scattered, and it took a moment or two for Slonský to register that the loud noise was actually two loud noises, each made by some kind of gun. Still unable to obtain a telephone signal, but his senses now fully focussed on the task in hand, he jogged in the direction of it.

The others had heard it too. Peiperová and Jerneková were furthest from it, but they briefly debated whether to cut

197

through the trees on the most direct bearing or to stick to the path. Peiperová decided that they should keep to the path because they would move more quickly, they would be able to see around themselves better, and it was where Rezek and Kašpar were most likely to be. They followed the first path they found to their left and moved forward at pace, their guns drawn and ready for use.

Navrátil and Krob had realised that they were likely to have been nearest to the source of the gunfire. Navrátil had suggested when they set off that they should separate by ten metres or so to make it harder for a gunman to shoot at them in quick succession, and this had enabled them to get a fairly good fix on the source of the noise. As they clambered upwards they came upon a small wooden shelter that had been constructed to allow walkers to take cover in the event of a storm. There was a sign on the door telling passers-by it was temporarily out of use, but Navrátil carefully opened the door. It was difficult to move because a sleeping bag and bedroll were pushed up against it, but eventually he forced it open, and found a man sitting against the rear wall. It was clear that this was the source of the shots because blood ran down the side of his face from a neat hole in his left temple. He was holding a gun in his right hand but it lay uselessly on the floor of the cabin.

'It's not Rezek, so I'm guessing it's Kašpar,' said Navrátil.

Krob was crouching outside, keeping watch. 'No chance it's suicide, I suppose.'

'Not unless he's a contortionist. His gun's in his right hand but he's been shot in the left side of the head. I was sure I heard two bangs, though.' Navrátil inspected the body more closely. 'It's been posed,' he decided. 'He's been shot in the back under the left shoulder blade. He probably dropped to the floor and was then finished off with a shot to the head. His gun was put in his hand afterwards, I expect.'

'He can't be far away. Let's leave Kašpar and get after him.'

'We ought to phone this in. Are you getting a signal?'

'No. How about you?'

'No. I guess we're not going to phone it in yet, then. Come on, same drill, ten metres apart whenever we can.'

Krob was scanning the path ahead. 'We'll have to go front and back rather than side by side over the next part. He didn't pass us going down, so let's assume he's planning to descend one of the other paths.'

'I just hope he isn't heading for the women,' said Navrátil.

Slonský had stepped off the path because he had spotted a rock that he could climb on get a better view. This meant that he would present an open target, but he was of the opinion that whoever had survived the duel must be on the upper path he could just see, and if they could pick him off at that distance they deserved a round of applause. The rock was an awkward shape, bulging in the middle but just a little too high for him to step on the outcrop to lever himself up, so he tried pulling himself up with his hands. It took a lot of effort, and he realised that it would have been a good idea to take his overcoat off when he left the car, but eventually he rolled onto the top and shaded his eyes with his hand to give him a better view.

Ahead of him he could see the trees leading up to a hill. There must have been some soil erosion because the middle third of the hill was bare of both soil and trees, at least in patches, and then there was a ledge that ran around the hill like a shelf before the hill resumed its upward tilt. From where Slonský was perched he could see that the hill had the appearance of a cone from which large spoons had gouged rock from the sides and front, with the result that the section directly in front of him was concave, forming an arc with the centre furthest from him, and hairpin corners to his left and right, that to his left being sharper than the one to his right.

Suddenly he saw movement in the bushes to the left and a small figure laboriously climbed up to the ledge and lifted himself up. Even at this distance, Slonský recognised Rezek, and dropped off the rock as quickly as he could to avoid being seen.

Below him he could see Dvorník following his route up the slope and signalled to him where Rezek was. Dvorník nodded, having seen the old man resting briefly on the ledge, and obeyed Slonský's instruction to head to the right to cut him off at the hairpin there. Slonský himself would cover the left hairpin.

Rezek looked exhausted by his activity thus far, and was not making a move in either direction at present, which suggested to Slonský that he and Dvorník should be able to trap him in a pincer. He might still try to shoot it out, but it would be stupid. On the other hand, Slonský had known an awful lot of stupid criminals in his time, and not all that many smart ones.

Navrátil and Krob had also gained the ledge path, Krob having suggested that if they ascended to it they might be looking down on Rezek amongst the greenery, so they were proceeding in single file, Navrátil in front, Krob ten metres behind and looking downwards whenever he could for any sign of their quarry.

At one point he saw movement below him and dropped to one knee to present a smaller target and get a better aim, whistling softly to Navrátil as he did so, but once the branches parted they could see it was Slonský below them, making heavy weather of scrambling up the rocks, seemingly oblivious to their presence.

They continued forward until they reached the bend in front of them. Navrátil rounded it carefully, his gun at shoulder height. He could see nobody in front of him and beckoned Krob forward.

Navrátil took two more steps and found himself facing Rezek, who had stepped out from a small niche and pulled his trigger. The bullet smacked into Navrátil's chest, followed by another a little lower, and he fell backwards on the path.

And stayed there.

Chapter 18

After the shots, there was a profound silence. The women ran forward to the bend in front of them. They could see a figure on the ground, Rezek backing away with his gun raised, and another figure stooped over the casualty, protecting him from further harm with his own body while trying to determine if there was any hope for him. The stooping man rolled the fallen one onto his side and stood up, at which point they knew him to be Krob.

Peiperová let out an anguished howl, redolent of pain and grief, and clasped her face in her hands, pulling them away in the forlorn hope that she had seen some kind of trick of the light. Unable to move, she crouched, shaking with sobbing, until Jerneková was able to pull her backwards by her shoulders and push her up against the rock around the corner.

'Leave this to me,' Jerneková told her. 'I'll get the bastard.'

She moved forward, dropping as low as she could to present the smallest possible target. On the other side Krob was inching forward cautiously. At one point he fired a shot to discourage Rezek from stepping out from his niche again, but Krob remained patient, refusing to let the desire for immediate revenge make him reckless. However long it took, he was not going to let Rezek escape them now.

Slonský had been too close to the hill face to see clearly what was happening on the ledge when the shots were fired, but now he had retreated to a better vantage point. He had seen Krob and Navrátil advancing, and had seen one of them fall, shot at not much more than twenty metres, but it was not until he recognised Krob inching forward that he realised it was his former trainee, his great hope, his surrogate son, who had been felled.

Rare indeed had been the times in Slonský's life when he had felt anything like the emotions that were now filling him. The loss of Navrátil left him empty; but he filled the space with rage.

'Rezek!' he bellowed. 'Your sorry arse is mine. Dead or alive, you're coming off this hill with me. That's a promise.'

Rezek answered with a couple of shots in Slonský's general direction. Slonský had been shot once in his career already — an event that he was always at pains to point out involved a ricochet, in view of where the bullet had lodged in his backside — and knew that being hit by a bullet did not always hurt as much as you might expect. He therefore paused for a second or two to check himself over before resuming his drive towards the old man who now realised that he was trapped unless he could kill Krob or the two women, and since Krob was clearly prepared to take his time about flushing Rezek out, the General decided that the women were the likelier option and began to make his way round the ledge towards them.

Jerneková remembered the order not to kill if possible, and fired at Rezek's knee. It chipped the rock beside him, close enough for him to realise that she was a better shot than he had expected, but he knew he was a good one too, and he backed himself to bring her within lethal range before she could stop him.

He reckoned without Dvorník, who had found a small soil-covered bank with a lateral tree branch on which he could steady his arm. As Rezek advanced with his gun drawn there was the crack of a shot and a bullet smacked into Rezek's forearm, causing him to drop his gun. It lay about two metres below the ridge but before he had the chance to get to it Krob had sprinted forward and grabbed him by the injured arm. In a fever of activity he cranked his handcuffs open and attached them to Rezek's right arm and his own left.

The old man was not prepared to show any pain from his wound. 'Go on,' he said to Krob. 'Finish me off. You know you want to.'

'I want to,' Krob agreed, 'but I follow orders. You're coming with me.'

'Am I?' said Rezek, ran two steps forward and jumped off the ledge. Too late, Krob realised his predicament. He just had time to drop his gun before his feet slipped over the edge.

It was not a sheer fall, but a steep, rocky slope littered with bushes and tree stumps. It was around one of these that Krob managed to hook his free arm, so that Rezek was dangling in the air from his other arm. If he had wanted, Rezek could have planted his feet on the soil but he kept his knees drawn up so that his whole weight was pulling Krob downward.

Slonský and Dvorník scampered sideways as fast as they could, each aiming to get underneath Rezek to take his weight before Krob's shoulder gave way, but they were beaten to it by Jerneková. Racing along the ledge she jumped into a bush to break her fall, then scooped Rezek's legs up with one arm. With her other she dipped into the pocket of her trousers to produce her handcuff key and deftly released Krob's wrist.

Rezek was still struggling to free his legs, but Jerneková's eyes met his, and he fleetingly glimpsed her smile as she let go of his legs and let him drop.

She pushed Krob upward so that he could get both arms on the stump then continued to force him up until she could get him safely on the ledge. It was clear that the episode had caused a good deal of damage to his shoulder, which hung limply at his side, and he was in considerable pain, but he gasped his thanks.

She had gone, chasing after Peiperová who was running towards Navrátil's body.

'Wait!' she yelled. 'Kristýna! Wait!'

But it was no good. Nothing was going to stop Peiperová running to embrace her fallen hero. She stumbled the last few metres, dropping to her knees and lifting his head so she could get an arm underneath it.

This was clearly Rezek's lucky day. Having been sent on his way by Jerneková, his downward progress had been arrested by Dvorník, whose bulk flopped on him with split-second timing. Since Slonský was wont to describe Dvorník as "large-framed", this abrupt deceleration did Rezek no good at all, and he was struggling to breathe under the weight of a hundred and twenty kilos of detective lieutenant when Slonský arrived, himself rather breathless, and gave the injured man a kick in the ribs for starters.

Dvorník was not moving until Rezek was secured, so Slonský fastened his own cuffs on Rezek's arms before using Dvorník's to pin Rezek's ankles either side of a thorny bush, giving Rezek a little shove so that his crotch nestled nicely against its trunk.

'If he moves, beat him ninety per cent dead,' Slonský ordered Dvorník.

'Let's call it ninety-five,' Dvorník replied.

As Slonský ascended to the ledge he could see Krob had joined the women and was blocking his view, but Peiperová was kneeling over Navrátil while Jerneková wrapped an arm around her shoulders. Krob was gesturing back along the path and

Slonský was surprised to see Jerneková suddenly break away and sprint as fast as she could away to his left.

Finally Slonský gained the ledge and made all speed to join them. 'Lass, I'm so, so sorry,' he began.

Peiperová turned to look at him, her blue eyes reddened with tears, her cheeks glistening with their trails. 'He's alive,' she whispered

'No, Kristýna, he was too close…'

'He is, sir,' Krob confirmed, and used his left arm to roll Navrátil onto his back. It was then that it registered with Slonský that both Krob and Navrátil were wearing bulletproof vests. The two bullets had ripped right into the vest but he could see very little blood around the holes. 'He hit his head when he fell back,' said Krob. 'That's why I turned him into the recovery position before I moved on.'

'Right! Let's get an ambulance for him double-quick.'

'That's where Lucie's gone, sir,' said Peiperová. 'She's a rough diamond, but she's a gem, sir. In her own way.'

Krob agreed. 'She saved me. I couldn't have held on much longer, sir.'

'Get yourself down that hill, lad, and get that shoulder seen to.'

Krob nodded. 'I don't mind admitting I could do with something for the pain.'

'I'm not surprised. That looks nasty. I'd better see if we can find Kašpar, I suppose.'

'He's in the hut, sir. Shot twice at close range.'

Slonský stood with his hands on his hips. 'Well, you seem to have sorted this all out very well for me. Let's get the casualties to hospital and Dvorník and I will take Rezek back to Prague and see how many times he falls out of our hands on the way to the interview room.'

Colonel Rajka insisted that either he or Major Lukas should be present during the interview to guard against any future accusations of brutality during questioning. He actually said "false accusations", but if Slonský had had his way there would have been nothing false about them.

Jerneková was sent to the canteen to fetch three coffees, one for each officer and one for the prisoner. Mucha saw her with the tray and held the door open for her.

'You thirsty?' he said.

'None of these are for me. One for Captain Slonský, one for Major Lukas, and one for the prisoner.'

'I'm sorely tempted to spit in his,' Mucha admitted.

'Don't bother,' Jerneková smiled. 'I already have.'

She pushed open the interview room door and handed the coffees around. As she left she found herself face to face with Colonel Rajka.

'You did well today, Officer Jerneková,' he said. 'I can see now why Slonský was so keen to have you joining his team.'

'Thank you, sir.'

'How long have you got left on your basic training?'

'Just one more week, sir.'

Rajka nodded, turned and began to walk away. 'See out that week, Jerneková, then I think you've done long enough in uniform. You can do your remaining rotations here. For form's sake we'll say it's six months with me, six with Lieutenant Dvorník and six with Captain Slonský, but so long as you keep your nose clean we can work around the formalities.'

'Thank you, sir,' Jerneková replied, and followed Rajka along the corridor. *He's not as big a tosser as I thought*, she mused to herself.

Slonský and Lukas had questioned suspects together many times in the past. Although each had now been elevated one rank, they quickly resumed their respective roles, Lukas being the good cop, keen on fairness and the integrity of the system, and Slonský threatening to obtain the confession he knew would eventually be forthcoming by being "persuasive", which he pronounced in such a way as to suggest to the unhappy prisoner that it might be a euphemism.

Rezek had been trained not to give up information, and neither officer believed that this was going to be easy. On the other hand, Rezek was proud of what he had done and was defiantly maintaining that any man would have done it too.

'I'm not talking about what you did today,' said Slonský.

'It's actually yesterday now,' murmured Lukas, pointing at his watch. 'Just to avoid confusion on the recording.'

'Quite right,' said Slonský, 'it is now 01:20, so the events to which I referred happened yesterday. But since I'm not talking about those let's press on, shall we? Let's go back to 1970 and the death of Tomas Kašpar. Incidentally, it's quite an achievement to murder a father and son thirty-eight years apart. There can't be many people who have done that.'

'I was an obedient servant of the State,' claimed Rezek. 'What I did was in accordance with my instructions at the time.'

'You're claiming you were ordered to kill him?' Lukas asked.

'No, I was ordered to use particular methods to obtain information, following which he died,' Rezek replied. 'There is a difference.'

'Is there?' Slonský snapped. 'You do something, you meant to do it, and someone died. Seems a pretty straightforward description of murder to me.'

'I had done it many times before. I was not to know that the young man we were questioning had a heart defect.'

'Unfortunately, the informality of your approach is going to make it quite hard for you to prove that you didn't know. And I can't imagine we'll find too many witnesses willing to come forward and support your claim that they withstood the voltage with no ill effects.'

'I don't doubt you can get a conviction,' Rezek sniffed. 'But my conscience is clear.'

'And Bartek and Toms? Had your experience taught you that if you do it right men can survive being shot in the back of the head at close range?'

'I was ordered to execute them. I am no more to be criticised than the members of a firing squad.'

'I see. But — and you'll correct me if I'm wrong — you were a General in the StB and deputy head of your section. Who could give you orders? I'd have thought a General had to be a bit of a self-starter, doesn't he?'

'Officers were required to show initiative at times, yes, but always within a framework of properly authorised orders laid down by competent authorities.'

'And who were these competent authorities of whom you speak?'

'The organs of the Party, of course. The Party and the State were one.'

'So when you shot Bartek and Toms, were you wearing your Party hat or your State hat?'

'Both.'

'And which one are you talking through now?'

Peiperová was surprised when the door opened and Jerneková walked in.

'It's after one o'clock,' she said. 'You should go home.'

'Hark who's talking,' Jerneková replied. 'At least I've had a wash and something to eat. How is he?'

'He's doing all right, thanks. He came round in the ambulance on the way to the hospital. They sent me outside while they check him over again. There's no bleeding in his brain, just a big lump on the back of his head, and a nasty bruise to his lower ribs where the second bullet hit him. The first one had enough force to go right through his vest and hit his chest, but it didn't penetrate far and he didn't bleed much from it.'

'I thought bulletproof vests were supposed to, you know, be proof against bullets.'

'Most of the time they are, but if you're that close, it's asking a lot of any garment to protect you.'

'It's lucky they went back to the car and put them on.'

'Jan insisted.'

Jerneková nodded. 'I'll never complain about how uncomfortable those things are again,' she said, 'even if they were designed by men who didn't allow for boobs.'

Peiperová was staring at the blank wall of the corridor. They passed some time in silence together, then Peiperová's face crumpled in tears once more. 'I don't know if I can go on doing this, Lucie. When I thought he was dead...' Her voice tailed away.

'When you thought he was dead — what?'

Peiperová wiped her eyes and blew her nose, trying to compose herself. 'I was thinking back to a case about eighteen months ago. An undercover officer was stabbed to death and I had to visit his widow. They had a little boy and I watched her trying to come to terms with it all and thought that I couldn't handle it as well as she was. I couldn't imagine kissing my husband goodbye and not knowing if he would come home again. And today, when Jan was shot, it all came back. Can I go on being a police officer and put myself through that?' She stopped and looked at Jerneková.

'Well, that's a load of crap for a start,' her junior told her.

'What?'

'You would have had the same feelings if you were in the police or out of it. It's not you being a police officer that's the problem, but him. He'd have been just as shot and you'd have been just as crushed if you were sitting at home unemployed. And take it from one who knows, being unemployed isn't all it's cracked up to be.'

Peiperová could not quite believe what she was hearing.

'And look at it from Jan's point of view,' Jerneková continued. 'Suppose Rezek had turned left instead of right. He'd have shot you and Jan would have had to come to terms with being without you. Do you think for one minute he'd be sitting here wittering on about giving it all up?'

'Probably not.'

'No, probably not. Thank you. I rest my case. Nothing is gained by either of you giving up your careers. The best thing you can do is get yourself promoted into a nice safe desk job as fast as you can. Majors and Colonels don't get shot on duty. We do.'

'I had a nice safe desk job,' Peiperová confided. 'I was bored to tears.'

'Well, there you are. Like somebody or other said once in some book I had to read at school, everything is for the best in the best of all possible worlds.'

'You really believe that?'

Jerneková considered for a while. 'Yes,' she said firmly, 'I think I do. I mean, look at what my life was like six months ago, and where I am now. I've got a secure job, I've got money in my purse, I've got a room to call my own, I've got prospects and I'm living in Prague rather than a suburb of a dead-end city made mainly of concrete. That's progress. And until yesterday you and Jan were living the dream. You're getting married — congratulations, by the way — and you've got a nice flat and a decent wage, you're both highly thought of and you're both good at what you do. Captain Slonský is taking bets on which of you two will make Director of Police first.'

'Is he? Who is his money on?'

'He won't say.'

Peiperová felt cheered by her colleague's comments, however unorthodox their expression. 'Do you know how Ivo and Hauzer are doing? Jan wasn't the only one hurt today, after all.'

'Hauzer's okay. They're keeping him in for observation only because he was unconscious for a while, but he was quite chirpy when I saw him earlier. Ivo's not so good. Taking Rezek's weight on his arm has done a lot of damage to his shoulder. They say he's going to need an exploratory operation tomorrow morning and then a prolonged period of physiotherapy to get his arm back in use. They're hoping the nerves weren't too badly damaged.'

'Poor Ivo. I didn't realise. I feel guilty now that I was obsessing about Jan when Ivo needed us.'

'You were doing what seemed right at the time. Ivo understands. They've given him some heavy duty stuff to deal with the pain.'

'Is he comfortable now?'

'I don't know about comfortable. The last I heard he was babbling about angels and fairies.'

'Must be good stuff,' Peiperová smiled.

'Has anyone told Jan's mother?'

Peiperová's hand flew to her mouth. 'Oh my God! I forgot all about her.'

'Don't worry. Let the poor woman get her sleep. I'll drop round in the morning if you give me her address.'

'It ought to be me. I'm the future daughter-in-law.'

'No, you'll be fast asleep if you've got any sense. Besides which, I'm a better liar than you. When I tell her he fell over and banged his head I'll be a lot more convincing than you will be.'

Chapter 19

Rajka was beginning to understand why people watched wildlife films. There was something impressive about the way that Slonský and Rezek were challenging each other in a display akin to two stags disputing ownership of the highest crag on the hillside.

Lukas and Slonský had finished questioning Rezek at 02:05. Slonský had retired to his office for a nap at his desk, and here they were at 08:23, ready to start again. Lukas had gone home to recover, so Rajka was now sitting in. He was no slouch at interrogation himself, and Slonský was very happy to let him lead on this session.

'Let us clarify exactly where we are,' said Rajka. 'You do not deny killing Tomáš Kašpar, Bartek and Toms, but claim that it was not murder because it was justifiable homicide.'

'Correct,' said Rezek. 'I was ordered to do it by legal authority.'

'That, of course, will be a matter for the courts to decide. But if I draw up a statement along the lines I have just described, you would be prepared to sign it?'

'Subject to any legal advice I might receive, yes,' agreed Rezek.

'You've waived your right to have a lawyer present,' Rajka pointed out.

'For the moment. Lawyers are expensive. There's no point in running up a bigger bill than necessary. I reserve the right to change my mind later.'

Rajka made a note. 'Very well. Let's park that for now. I want to turn to what happened after the death of your daughter. How did František Kašpar contact you?'

'I managed to discover his address and went to see him. The bird had flown, but there was a letter addressed to me on the table. It contained an admission that he had murdered my daughter and that, after leaving me to suffer my loss for a while, he was going to come after me.'

'Do you still have that letter?'

'I burned it.'

'But it contained details of yesterday's rendezvous?'

'Yes. It told me to be at a particular point at two in the afternoon.'

'I don't understand that,' Slonský remarked. 'Why would he tell you where he was going to kill you?'

'He was conceited enough to think he could outwit me, I suppose. But the ostensible reason was so that he could question me about his father. He said if I came unarmed and discussed what happened with him he would undertake to give me a quarter of an hour's start before he came after me. That suggested to me that the final meeting point was to be at least fifteen minutes' walk from the car park.'

'But you didn't go unarmed,' Slonský followed up.

'Of course not. I'm not an idiot. And I had no intention of giving this insect any explanation at all. My plan was to get to the park at least three hours earlier and look for him. Plainly he wasn't going to risk meeting in the car park. Besides, he would need some time for his preparations.'

'Preparations?'

'My instructions were to follow the path to a particular tree. There would be a chalked R for Rezek and an arrow to tell me which way to go next. Follow the signs and I would reach the meeting point.'

'I didn't see any signs,' Slonský remarked, 'so presumably we all arrived before he had time to set them up.'

'A beginner's mistake,' Rezek scoffed. 'I saw it many times in my professional life. I hadn't wasted the intervening days. I'd obtained detailed maps of the trails and I'd learned the terrain as well as I could.'

'You were being watched,' said Slonský. 'You rarely left your house.'

'There's such a thing as mail order,' Rezek remarked. 'It seemed to me that if he had chosen this place it was probably somewhere he knew well, and there was likely to be a place where he could prepare himself, and perhaps stow some valuables. Have you found his father's bones yet?'

'Not yet,' Slonský admitted.

'They weren't in his flat. He'll have stashed them somewhere safe. If they're not in his backpack they'll be in a left luggage office, I expect. Anyway, once I realised these huts were dotted around the park I knew where he'd be. He wouldn't use one of the big ones because he might have company there, so he'd find a nice small one and make sure nobody else wanted to share it. When I walked up the path and saw a sign on the door that said the hut was out of use while it was being refurbished I guessed that was the one. There are enough cracks in the planking to look inside. He was checking over his gun, the gun with which he intended to kill me. I just pushed the door open and fired. He dropped to his knees and I put him out of his misery. Then I sat him against the wall and put the gun back in his hand.'

'So you admit killing František Kašpar?' Rajka interrupted.

'Certainly. I'm sure you'll have forensic evidence proving that it was my gun. But I do not deny anything. However, it was justifiable homicide.'

'In what way was it justifiable?'

'The law recognises a right to self-defence. He had threatened to kill me, not in general terms but in a specific place at a particular time. Killing him a couple of hours earlier was simply defending myself. He had the gun in his hand. He could have shot me at that very moment. There was an imminent threat. And given how ineptly he handled his gun, I deserve some thanks for preventing a shootout in some public place where a passer-by might have been killed.'

Rajka could see Slonský becoming incensed and suggested that this would be a good time to take a break, during which Rezek's arm could be examined by a doctor, and then bundled Slonský outside.

'Let it go. He's slowly sinking in his own quicksand,' Rajka ordered.

'If I hear that phrase "justifiable homicide" one more time I'm very likely to take a leaf out of his book and justifiably ram his gun where he'll have a hell of a problem reaching the trigger.'

'We'll give him a couple of hours to stew, then we'll charge him with the attempted murder of Navrátil and Krob. If nothing else that will allow us to keep him in custody pending trial.'

Slonský's eyes were still blazing, but he could do nothing more; perhaps his anger arose from the very fact that he could do nothing more. 'I'll go and check how the men are doing in hospital,' he said at length. 'And I'd better see how Peiperová is too. She was very shaken by the events of yesterday.'

'You do that. I can wrap up here and no doubt Officer Jerneková would be happy to sit in on the interview in your place.'

Officer Jerneková was busy reading a textbook on investigative methods while she ate her lunch, this being achieved by spearing pickles in a jar with her penknife and taking bites from slices of dry bread.

'How are the casualties?' Slonský enquired.

'Navrátil is likely to be released this evening, sir. They've found nothing amiss, even when they did one of those special x-rays that slices your head in all directions. I visited his mother this morning to let her know what was going on and I think she's insisting he stays with her to recuperate.'

'How does Peiperová feel about that?'

'She needs some time to think about her own position, she says. It's all right, I've told her she's being a drip and I think she's coming round. After all, most of the murder victims we see didn't think they were in any kind of danger, did they? So you can't say you're safer doing one job than another. Anyway, she's got a wedding and a flat to take her mind off it.'

'I hope that works. I'd hate to lose her.'

'You won't. If she shows signs of leaving I'll just call her a quitter. She'll stay to prove me wrong.'

Slonský allowed himself a thin smile. Jerneková and tact were strangers to each other. 'How about Krob?'

'Not so good, I'm afraid. They've had to repair several badly torn muscles. The nerves were damaged but they think they'll repair in time. For now they've had to immobilise his shoulder until everything knits, then he'll need a lot of physiotherapy. It's going to be a long haul for him. But he'll get there. He's very patient, isn't he?'

'Yes, he is,' agreed Slonský.

'And Hauzer will go home today too, sir. Bit of a sore head and he needed a few stitches, but he'll be all right.'

Slonský thanked her for the update and decided he needed some thinking time, not to mention some cogitation lubricant, so he grabbed his hat and coat and went off in search of a consoling glass.

The next few days were very strange. Slonský had been in places where a colleague had been killed and he knew the blanket of gloom that descends and quietens the office, the things that people think and do not want to voice aloud, the glances at the empty chair; now he pushed open the door of the men's office and looked at the two unoccupied desks and it seemed natural to sigh. He walked to the women's office and saw another empty desk because he had given Peiperová some compassionate leave.

Jerneková looked up from her notepad where she was drafting her report on the discovery of Tomáš Kašpar's bones in a left luggage locker. Though she was perfectly competent on a computer she liked to marshal her thoughts on paper first.

'It's just thee and me now, Jerneková,' Slonský said.

'The criminals of Prague should be quaking, sir,' she said. 'We can cope. But I'm on my period so I'm less tolerant than usual.'

Ten out of ten for openness, thought Slonský, *and a big fat zero for self-awareness.*

He returned to his own desk and reflected that for nearly all his life he had been very happy working alone, then Lukas had given him an ultimatum; if you don't want to be retired, take on a trainee. And Navrátil appeared.

He was a breath of fresh air. Suddenly there was someone who hung on Slonský's every word, including his worst jokes and his most self-aggrandizing accounts of past glories. To his surprise he found there were other scrupulously honest cops out there, and some of them were ferociously bright. Navrátil learned quickly, and their relationship was changing. Now Navrátil gave as well as received. If he thought Slonský was wrong, he wasn't afraid to say so.

And in another challenge to Slonský's previous thinking, he had found a woman who enhanced the team. Peiperová had a gift for organisation. He had lost count of the number of times she had reminded him of tasks he had forgotten, birthdays he needed to remember, little things in witness statements that needed to be followed up. On top of that, there seemed to be no office gadget she could not work better than he could. She photocopied the right side of a piece of paper, managed to listen to answerphone messages without wiping them first, and regularly showed him things his mobile phone could do that he had never suspected. Admittedly his first attempt to fly solo had misfired a little; when he tried to order a pizza delivery, he accidentally typed 11 instead of 1 and made himself very popular with the night shift by sharing them around, but he would never have tried that had it not been for her.

Then there was Krob, who was Slonský's exact opposite. Patient, gentle, methodical, all the things that Slonský was not. Another thoroughly decent young man whose future may just have been made much more difficult by a disabling injury. It had never crossed Slonský's mind that Rezek might be so full of bile and hate that he would jump off a ledge handcuffed to an officer. It made him all the more determined to see Rezek behind bars for the rest of his life.

And what about Jerneková? Mucha, who knew him better than Slonský was prepared to admit, had been heard to describe Lucie as Slonský with a bust. He hoped that wasn't true, because even he had more social skills than she had. Hadn't he?

He was shaken out of his daydream by the telephone ringing. It was the Prosecutor's Office. Slonský listened in increasing disbelief as the Assistant Deputy Under-Prosecutor or some such nonentity explained that they did not propose to charge Rezek with the 1970 killings, nor with any harm caused to Krob, but were going to concentrate on the killing of František Kašpar and the wounding of Navrátil, though even this had been downgraded to the lowest category. Slonský listened without comment, checked the name of the caller, and then stormed along the corridor to see Rajka.

Rajka was equally indignant though unsurprised. 'I sometimes think Hitler could have got away with a suspended sentence from our prosecutors. It's a nonsense, but our choice is simple. We settle for a quiet life and accept it, or we go and argue our case.'

'I agree,' said Slonský. 'Are you going to drive?'

'The problem is,' said Prosecutor Janák, 'that we have insufficient evidence to charge him with the three murders in 1970.'

'Except a confession,' said Slonský. 'That seems pretty substantial to me.'

'He'll probably repudiate that in court,' Janák replied.

'Well, of course he'll repudiate it,' Slonský told him. 'Every criminal always does. But the court usually says that's tough and stands by the original.'

Janák sighed. 'The other problem is that we're worried about his argument that his actions were legal at the time.'

'Surely that's for a court to decide?' said Rajka.

'Goodness, no!' Janák replied. 'That's the last thing we want. So long as a court hasn't taken a view on it, we're all right, but if they accept his submission everyone will be sheltering behind it.'

'Here's a thought,' Slonský said. 'Suppose we put it to the court and they come down on our side. Wouldn't that be a good thing?'

'But they might not,' Janák pointed out.

'And if you never put the question to them there's no point in prosecuting anyone for crimes under the old regime,' Slonský argued. 'They can always say it was authorised then, even if it's not true, because I have no idea how we would disprove it.'

'Look,' said Janák with a faint yet condescending smile, 'why are you so worried? The killing of František Kašpar alone is going to put him behind bars for the rest of his life.'

'I wouldn't put it past your lot to cock that up too and get it ruled a suicide,' Slonský replied with feeling.

Rajka intervened. 'It also does not reflect the deliberate wounding of two of my detectives, in one of whom we can make a very strong case for a charge of attempted murder.'

Janák checked his folder. 'Ah yes — Lieutenant Navrátil, wasn't it? But the difficulty there is that his injuries turned out to be relatively trivial. Rezek couldn't have foreseen that Navrátil would fall over and knock himself out.'

'Couldn't he?' said Slonský. 'Was Rezek entitled to assume that someone he shot would remain standing, then? Or perhaps we have to conduct a health and safety assessment on the way down to the ground so we don't hurt ourselves?'

'Your line of argument,' Rajka added, 'suggests that we should tell officers to leave off their bulletproof vests because that will determine the charges their assailants face.'

'As for poor Krob,' Slonský raged, 'are we to tell him his serious injury was just an accident?'

'From the statements it appears that Rezek was trying to commit suicide,' Janák remarked. 'He did not necessarily intend any harm to Krob.'

'He knew he was handcuffed to the poor lad,' said Slonský. 'Even you must admit that it's foreseeable that if you jump off a cliff handcuffed to some other poor bastard it's not going to end well for them.'

'His lawyer will argue that the balance of his mind was disturbed and therefore he wasn't responsible for his actions,' Janák replied.

'In that event, neither am I,' said Slonský, who stood up, walked round the desk and yanked Janák out of his seat, frogmarching him to the door and through the swing doors to the landing, where he proceeded to lift him bodily and push his upper half over the handrail at the top of the stairs. 'Look down,' he ordered.

'It's five floors!' yelped Janák.

'There's nobody down there. If I throw you off and you land on someone and kill them, is that my fault?' Slonský asked.

'Of course. It would be murder.'

'Right, foreseeable damage to another; that's my argument about Krob,' Slonský told him. 'If I hold you over the stairwell and your jacket rips and you fall to your death, is that my fault?'

'Yes! Yes!'

'But if you had different equipment you'd suffer different injuries. That's my argument about Navrátil. If I had thrown you over last week instead of today, would it have been less blameworthy?'

'No!'

'So an offence is the same whenever it was committed, which is my argument about the three killings in 1970.' Slonský pulled Janák to his feet. 'I'm glad we agree,' said Slonský. 'No doubt you'll revise your decisions.'

Janák straightened his suit and glared at Rajka. 'Have you no control over your officers?'

'I agree with him,' said Rajka. 'It seemed to me that Captain Slonský made his arguments clearly and cogently.'

'He could have dropped me,' whined Janák.

'I could,' conceded Slonský. 'But I didn't intend to, and according to you that makes all the difference.'

Janák made a formal complaint about Slonský's conduct to the Director of Police, Colonel Urban, who responded that the police service stood squarely behind Slonský. Janák then made a complaint to the Office of Internal Control, the OVK, which was the new name for the department that Rajka used to run. Major Lukas waited a week and then replied that after a full investigation they had been unable to find any matter worthy of reproach. Coincidentally, Valentin's newspaper ran an exposé into the workings of the Prosecutor's office in which it alleged that Klement Rezek, recently jailed for forty-two years for four murders and two attempted murders, was originally going to be charged with only one and questioned whether the department was fit for purpose. It also noted that one of the Prosecutor's staff had made "hysterical and unsubstantiated allegations" against a senior policeman to deflect attention from the department's shortcomings.

'That's good stuff,' said Slonský, lobbing the newspaper onto the table in front of them.

'I thought so,' agreed Valentin. 'So did my editor. Thanks for the exclusive.'

'One for the road?'

'Why not? You can add a plum brandy if you like.'

Epilogue

On Saturday, 21st June 2008, on a sunny afternoon in Kladno, Kristýna Peiperová, lieutenant in the Czech police service, married Lieutenant Jan Navrátil. As they left the church colleagues formed a guard of honour, the places nearest the church being taken by Officers Krob and Jerneková.

Krob had left off his sling for the occasion. Although his recently unused arm was weak, he had sensation in it and was able to use it to raise his glass in repeated toasts. Jerneková had agreed to take Slonský's phone calls during the ceremony and wedding breakfast in case he was needed, and ensured that he was not by turning it off as soon as she was given it. Captain Josef Slonský gave a brief but elegant speech in which he wished the young couple well and took credit for the way they had developed over the last couple of years. As he ended he said he wanted to be serious for a moment and express publicly the belief that the Czech public could be confident that in the two officers beside him the police service would be in good hands.

'I hope you have a wonderful honeymoon,' he said, 'and you'll be back at work at 7 a.m. on that Monday morning or I'll want to know why.'

As he sat down Peiperová leaned towards him. 'I wouldn't want to be anywhere else,' she said.

A NOTE TO THE READER

Dear Reader,

For those who like to know these things, this plot was actually the first of the series to be developed, but I put it aside to write *Lying and Dying* and only came back to it when I had completed *A Second Death.*

The starting point was the feeling that it would be difficult for the police to find a motive for a killing if the reason for committing it was not anything that the victim had done other than being connected with someone else.

I am gratified that readers take such an interest in my detectives, especially their lives outside work. Including some back story for some and a few day-to-day events for others helps to lighten the darkness that would otherwise be unavoidable due to the unpleasantness of the crimes I write about. It seems to me that a detective novel that concentrated entirely on some of these would be too depressing to enjoy. I took the risk of widening the cast a little, which seemed a natural progression; few of us work with the same individuals for many years without one or two changes.

Slonský is not yet ready to retire. I think if I tried to stop he would write the stories himself. So long as there is an appetite for reading about his activities I hope to keep going!

There are two potential cliff-hangers here I ought to sort out. On Saturday, 21st June 2008, on a sunny afternoon in Kladno, Kristýna Peiperová, lieutenant in the Czech police service, married Lieutenant Jan Navrátil. As she left for her honeymoon she promised Slonský she would be back at her desk in a fortnight. Behind her Slonský could see Lucie

Jerneková mouthing "Told you so".

If you have enjoyed this novel I'd be really grateful if you would leave a review on **Amazon** and **Goodreads**. The best salesmen for my books are readers, so please tell your friends too! I love to hear from readers, so please keep in touch through **Facebook** or **Twitter**, or leave a message on my **website**.

Všechno nejlepší!

Graham Brack

Sapere Books is an exciting new publisher of brilliant fiction and popular history.

To find out more about our latest releases and our monthly bargain books visit our website: **saperebooks.com**

Printed in Great Britain
by Amazon